NOT
A
BAD
MAN

WILLIAM MORROW AND COMPANY, INC.

NEW YORK   1978

NOT A BAD MAN

A NOVEL BY

JOHN MIGLIS

All characters in this book are fictitious, and any resemblance to actual persons, living or dead, is purely coincidental.

———————————

Library of Congress Cataloging in Publication Data

Miglis, John.
    Not a bad man.

    I. Title.
PZ4.M6316Th 1978 [PS3563.I3715] 813'.5'4
ISBN 0-688-03258-3   77-24636

BOOK DESIGN   CARL WEISS

FOR

ERNESTINE,

LOVE

OF MY LIFE

Wei chi / Before Completion

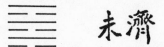

The hexagram *Before Completion* represents a transition from chaos to order. This hexagram comes at the end of the Book of Changes. It points to the fact that every end contains a new beginning. Thus it gives hope to men.

—From a note by Richard Wilhelm
in his translation of
The I Ching

CHAPTER

PAUL MCGAVIN SAT UNCOMFORTABLY IN DONNY'S PINK OVER-
stuffed chair, fingering his third Scotch and soda. In the
irregularly shadowed light of the cabin, he examined the Audubon painting of a great blue heron that hung on the
wall beside him. The heron he had seen on the Ocklawaha
trip with the Group had not looked like that at all. This one
stood gray and angular in the saw grass; its bushy head was
stiff; its eyes were distant and lifeless; while the one he had
seen that morning—seen leap from an ocean of hyacinths in
a deafening flurry of silver-blue wings, pumping close to the
glassy surface and away—had been as smooth and graceful as
a dancer. For nearly an hour it had flown ahead of their
canoe, like a guide, settling for as long as it took them to
catch up, and then leaping again. They had all considered
it a good sign.

The painting wasn't even close. But so many things had turned out differently than they were supposed to. Across the room, a huge dark oak table intruded on the delicate order of things. It was strewn with manila legal folders and expensively bound law texts. Underneath, the massive oak legs were powdered white with dust.

There was something in the familiar arrangement of things that bothered him. It was almost as if he could faintly smell his wife's perfume still in the air. He was certain that she had moved around this room, straightened the magazines on the coffee table, perhaps even swept the pressed pinewood floor. Donny was not capable of these things.

He had suspected the two of them for nearly a month. He wanted to say something to Donny, trick him in some rhetorical way into admitting that they had been carrying on. He had to hear the words. But every time he felt he had constructed an adequate trap, he became scared, and his voice held enough of a tremble to betray him. After all, you didn't go around accusing a man like Donald "Donny" Waldo of sleeping with your wife. He'd tear you to pieces.

Donny came striding into the room, his heels clacking the floor, stirring a drink. "If Owen wasn't with you," he said, "I'da never believed it."

"What I saw wasn't uncommon at all."

"You probably bullied that rabbit of a kid into vouching for your story." Donny laughed, then sat at the table. He picked up one of his manila folders and flipped it open.

Bullying's your style, Paul thought. "Crosby'll tell you, or anybody that knows anything about eagles. What I saw wasn't at all uncommon." He sat a full fifteen feet across the room, and yet he felt Donny's eyes hard on him, as though he were on a witness stand being cross-examined. It was hard trying to maintain any civility with a man who constantly held you on trial. It was doubly hard if you thought he was sleeping with your wife.

10

He saw Donny's sharp features in silhouette, etched against the bright afternoon light that poured in from the window behind him. His head was small, squared-off at the forehead and chin. It was joined to his wide shoulders by an almost petite neck. "What time are they going to get here?" Paul asked.

"Don't know. I oughta be doing some of this work though," Donny tapped the folder in his hands, "instead of holding this meeting today."

"It was your idea. Why the hell do you call them, then bitch about the time you're wasting?" It was the Group's joke. If Donny said he'd give you three minutes of his life, you could time an egg by it.

"Just the same," Donny said flatly, "I can't picture it. I never heard of an eagle running from anything other than a man. And here *you* are," he squeezed off the word from where he sat, "proposing to our group of exceptionally sane and reasonable men that you saw one run from an osprey." He looked down at the folder dramatically, as if he had just finished his closing argument.

"You're just like the kid," Paul said. "You have these romantic notions about eagles. They're just birds."

"Not quite." A sarcastic edge honed his voice. "They're the highest form of bird."

The rigid way Donny sat reminded Paul of a stonecutting jutting through the dreamy quality of unfocused light that suffused the room. The soft edges of light made his face nearly blacked in shadows; his nose curved small and angular like a beak. What did she see in him? His was a common handsomeness. Paul drained his glass, and asked Donny for another drink. He was getting progressively drunker, and he could smell Lorene's scent as strongly as if she were there herself. Clouds of it swirled around Donny's silhouette.

There was a pink and green pastel hue to the clouds. He imagined both her and Donny in the back bedroom. He could hear her buoyant voice singing Donny's name, and heard him answer her. But Donny was still sitting there, and words were tumbling from his mouth. The green-eyed monster.

Donny was saying, "I'm just trying to elicit the facts." There was a maddeningly regular ticking to his voice. "That is an attorney's stock in trade, the skillful manipulation . . ."

"I don't care about your job. At least I've had another sighting." He wanted to catch the words as they came out, but they rolled uncontrollably off his thick tongue. His ears burned, and he said, "Get me that other drink, will you?"

"Paul, Paul, Paul," Donny sang. "You sound like a twelve-year-old. What's eatin' at you?"

And you sound like somebody's mother. "Nothing," he said.

Donny took his glass and went into the kitchen. That skinny bastard knows. He smiled to himself as he mixed Paul's drink, and he thought of Lorene lying naked out there on the dock that first day, her nipples as big as cocktail coasters, the pinkness blending gradually with her large flattened breasts. It was poetic the way the sun caught in the fine hair of her firm stomach, like a yellow mist. He'd tried to move on her, and she had stopped him. "I want to tan," she had said. "Forget it." And he had lain there beside her with his erection painfully pressed into the planking, remembering the night he had watched her dance in Dallas.

Now Paul was out there, in his living room, fuming his mad little brains out. He did not need the shit Paul was capable of dredging up. Not with the elections on Tuesday. The trial tomorrow before that motherfucker Eastmund. But he found himself drawn into his passionate scenario anyway. He did not hate Paul, nor even despise him as he thought he should. He merely used him to keep something deep inside him pumping. This wasn't the only time either, but it was the time he needed trouble the least. He could feel the pressure steadily rising inside his head; he knew there had to be a confrontation sooner or later. He would not let Paul get the best of him by any means. He mixed a double Scotch and soda.

When he came back in the room he said, "I don't mean to sound like I'm disputing you, Paul. Why don't you take it easy on the booze?"

Eat it, Paul thought. "Thanks," he said as he took the glass. He thought of his trip to the Audubon House near Mallory Square in Key West, and what a sham it all was. He squirmed under Donny's patronizing attitude. He *had* been to Lake Wauberg that day. He *had* seen it, and he did have the kid to corroborate his story.

He had picked up Owen at the hospital, insisting to the nurse that he be allowed to wheel him out, and that Owen was a hero, of sorts, for what he had tried to do.

"Maybe," the young nurse had said. She was a livid, sunburned pink, dressed in starched whites, and she crackled when she walked. "Though some people might say he was a fool," she giggled. She adjusted the sling on Owen's arm.

"That's no way for a nurse to talk about her patient," Owen had said.

"Former patient," she corrected him.

Paul shot her a glare. She winked at him as they walked out the lobby and across the white-hot sidewalk to Paul's car.

"It's ok," Owen said to Paul. "She was just kidding."

"I don't blame your son for what he did," she said.

"He's not my son. He's my student."

"Oh, I thought . . ."

Paul raised his hand to silence her.

"Anyway," she continued, hardly missing a beat, "it was pretty romantic if you ask me. And dumb too." She laughed, and Paul felt outside some joke they had between them.

Owen pushed out of the chair, and hugged her with his free arm. "I'll give you a call about next weekend, ok?"

"Sure," she said. "And don't forget to change that dressing like the doctor showed you."

He touched the gauze bandage that wrapped around his forehead and bulged over his left eye. "That's not the sort of thing you forget."

Then they had driven out Highway 441, an asphalt ribbon that cut through Paines Prairie, and turned up the long driveway to the lake. Clusters of scrub palmettos and pines rimmed the perimeter of the recreation area. The saw grass and thick underbrush had been cleared from the lakeside and replaced with a neat rug of sod. A few greased college kids in bathing suits dodged tree stumps and tossed frisbees.

Across the lake, the vegetation was as dense and original as when the Seminoles had lived in the area. In the stands of tall cypress and slash pines, Paul had seen an unusually dark configuration that he had taken for a nest.

They sat on the hot planking of the dock, and he used his binoculars to scan the far side of the lake. Owen shaded his eye with his right hand and tried to draw into his vision any movement at all at treetop level.

A couple of sunbathers, glinting like brown metal, lay on towels behind them. The "Swap and Shop" voice on their radio drawled on endlessly about items for sale. Then tinny guitar twangs, accompanied by the nasal voices of country gentlemen, evaporated in the heat that rose from beneath the dock.

First, all they saw were ospreys circling high above the center of the lake. Paul marked the large fish hawks by their white underbellies and the conspicuous black wristbands on the crook of their wings.

He focused on a wall of gray-barked cypress on the far side of the lake. He drew the trees clearly into vision, and then began to tilt the glasses progressively higher, working the sky above them. Finally, he had the glasses at a sharp angle above his head. "Would you look at that?"

"What is it?" Owen asked.

"The biggest goddamned osprey I've ever seen. Five-and-a-half-foot wingspan if it's an inch."

He followed the bird as it circled and soared, as if on a rail that spiraled evenly and constantly upward. The sun burned at his forehead. The pale skin of his face felt as if it were drying out and beginning to sizzle. A stiff wind rippled the water, making it lap rhythmically against the pilings.

Soon the bird was only an outline against the white, searing sky. Then it began to stoop. It folded its wings, and like a sack of rocks, plummeted.

"Jesus, Owen, it's after something."

Just before it came level with the treetops, it pulled up and began furiously pumping its long sleek wings. Paul pulled the glasses out in front of the bird. "It's an eagle," he said. "The osprey's after a goddamned eagle."

Paul rose and tramped excitedly across the sunbathers' towels. "Come on, man," one of them said, pulling himself from a fried stupor. The other turned off the radio, and except for Paul's voice, there was instantaneous silence.

"I can't believe it. I can't believe I'm seeing this."

Owen said, "Let me see." He reached for the glasses, but Paul would not give them up.

The sunbathers pulled their towels from underneath Paul's feet. The osprey closed on the eagle, and it looked like a dogfight between two planes. As the osprey was about to reach the eagle's tail feathers, the eagle pulled its wings up slightly, and lifted on the air. The osprey shot underneath, and the eagle dropped down behind him.

Then the osprey pulled the same maneuver, and again chased the eagle. Finally the eagle dipped close to the water and pumped its broad sturdy wings. Paul thought he had seen water lift in that first sweep of air. He saw what Crosby, the old-timer of the Group, had talked about at their meetings: the power of the eagle.

The image froze in his mind like a photograph, like a vision. When the eagle pumped away from the osprey, it banked so that Paul had an overview of his topside. He saw a tautly muscled, brown body between the brilliant white head and tail. Then it was gone. In a blink. It could have disappeared for all he knew. Crosby had said something about that too. The osprey remained in his field of vision, but the eagle became, in a single sweep, a black line against the sky.

Owen finally pulled the glasses from Paul. Quickly focusing them, he said, "It was an eagle all right."

Paul wanted to tell him that he knew that already, that he was not a fool, and that it was unmistakable, but he did not want to talk to the kid that way. Just the same, he was thankful Owen had been there. Donny would no doubt grill the shit out of him. He began to form images in his head to express the magnificence of what he had seen for when it was his turn to tell the Group.

"Let's go have a drink," he said. "To celebrate."

"I'd rather smoke a joint," Owen said. "I've been dying to get high since I've been in the hospital."

Paul felt good, and so he said, "Why don't we do both?"

After they finished a joint in the car, they stopped at McElvay's Fish Camp for a beer. They sat in the shade of a cabbage palm, watching the Hobie Cats tack back and forth across the immense lake, their multicolored sails puffed full in the wind. The air was warm and they giggled from the pot and worked on a six-pack of Pabst. Paul kept saying, "I'll never see anything like it again, ever," as though he had seen Lazarus. Owen agreed, "You certainly were lucky."

It happened three times before they both realized that they were stuck, and they started laughing.

And now, sipping his Scotch while the shadows deepened in Donny's cabin, Paul had the strangest sensation that Donny was trying to strip him of the pleasure of his day. Owen had called it that. He said the next meeting of the Group would be Paul's day. Like a holiday or something. He had always had the suspicion that Donny embellished his own stories to compete with the others. He never saw a plain eagle; it was always doing some strange and marvelous thing.

Paul found himself telling Donny, "It's not that an eagle ran from an osprey; it's more like he didn't want to be bothered by him. He could have turned and minced him with his talons if he wanted to. But he didn't. That's power." He wanted to make Donny feel stupid. He wanted to say, you don't know shit from shinola when it comes to birds.

"Let's talk about something else," Donny said.

Let's talk about my wife, Paul thought. He knew something was about to happen between him and Lorene—those imprecise signs were beginning to show. Like the long-distance calls to Dallas. She had told him once that she didn't think she could break with her past. He had never forgotten it.

And she did not make love with him. She had fucked him, of course, but the intensity of their lovemaking had diminished until he had become convinced that she was not really interested anymore. During one of their mid-afternoon sessions, he had seen it in her eyes. They were so distant she could have been reading a book over his shoulder, except that she did not like to read.

There was Donny's cabin too. He had smelled her almost as soon as he had walked in the door. It was a shock that coursed through him, made his breathing rapid and high in his chest. It was not her perfume, but more the undefinable, yet unmistakable fragrance of her hair, that thick, well-cared-for red mane, the smell that carried him through the vague moments of post-lovemaking satisfaction.

He had smelled it in the arm of the couch when Donny had left to fix him his second drink, or third. Of that he was not sure. But he was sure that she had laid her head there. He buried his face in the arm of the couch, then slowly, sniffing like a hound dog, traced the outline of her head.

Next he began madly sniffing anything he thought would hold a scent. The back of the couch, the curtains, the chair by the window. He went back and smelled the arm of the couch again. Donny had come back in with the drinks, and he had asked Paul what in the hell he was doing.

"Smelling," he said as he got up and walked back to the overstuffed chair. He slumped into it.

"What?"

"Nothing."

He looked at the arrangement of things in the room. The books on the bookshelves were placed neatly, according to size, and comparing it with the clutter on the table, he concluded that Donny was incapable of such order. He had asked if he had a cleaning woman coming in once in a while. "Nope," Donny had said.

A fan of magazines was delicately laid out too, exactly as they were on his coffee table at home, with her favorite sticking out like a face card. It was all, and he thought Donny would really appreciate this, it was all an accumulation of circumstantial bullshit. Nevertheless . . .

Donny had changed to his only other topic of conversation: local politics and Tuesday's election. It was a special election to fill the House seat left vacant by the death of one of Putnam County's old-timers. Donny asked, "You gonna work the election for me?"

Paul suggested they go out on the porch. "I'd like to," he

lied. "But I'm going to be tied up in faculty meetings."

"I need all the help I can get."

In the light of the porch, brilliant from the reflection of the lake not more than a hundred feet away, Paul watched Donny's fierce eyes squint. "How about it?" he said again. Paul could feel his gaze pressing on him. A ridge raised along Donny's forehead, like the bony protuberance of a hawk. Paul was ready for Donny to shriek, then raise a tuft of feathers on the back of his neck in display. "Well?"

He almost offered Lorene's help to take himself off the spot. "I wish I could get away," he said finally.

He propped his feet on Donny's desk, which took almost the entire length of the porch. Fishing rods hung between the cross-supports of the dust-darkened screen, with colored worms dried to their hooks. There were topographical maps on all three walls, posters of fresh- and salt-water fish, artificially posed with incredulous two-dimensional stares, and an antique floor lamp arching up between two rocking chairs.

The cabin itself was secluded in a stand of slash pines. Some of the trees had been cleared before Donny rented the property from Crosby, making the smallest suggestion of a yard. Black oaks, sweet gums and turkey oaks thick as a rain forest walled the farthest banks of the lake.

"Since I've stopped the Howard Lake dredging," Donny said, "I've picked up the old-timers' votes and the Bass Club's votes. They don't want this area divided up for mobile homes for retired Yankees. C'mere, let me show you something." He pointed to a small lake on one of his topographical maps. "You shoulda been there. The bastard pulled in right about there." He stabbed his index finger at the pale blue ellipse. "With a backhoe. He started raking out the vegetation. You know how sound's amplified out here. Well, when I heard that machine going, I knew it wasn't the Kaolite mines."

Paul was only half listening. Nothing bored him more

than politics. He looked at Donny, but his eyes began to wander with his thoughts. There was a daybed in the corner of the porch. Its covers were rumpled. He thought if he felt it, the mattress would be warm. He wanted to nail the sonofabitch to the wall, like those vacant-eyed fish. Take him apart and be done with it. But he knew how difficult it would be.

He watched Donny's short, hard body as he paced in front of him. His shoulders were wide as a wedge. Outside, the air was still. Occasionally a breeze blew across the water, carrying warm humid air to the porch.

"Come on outside, and help me start the barbecue," Donny said.

Paul sat at the weathered, shaky picnic table. Donny poured charcoal into the barbecue pit, a fifty-five-gallon drum cut in two with reinforcing steel rods welded to the underbelly as legs. "The s.o.b. on the backhoe said he had a right, and I told him I'd slap a lawsuit on him faster than he could fart." He piled the coals and drenched them with fluid. "He stopped, but I didn't know if I had a leg to stand on. I looked it up in the state statute books. Nothing. Then I found something in the federal books."

Donny was always making speeches, ever since he had taken the notion to run for office. Even if he was to give you directions to somewhere, it sounded like a speech.

"I don't want to talk politics," Paul blurted. It came out before he could stop it.

Donny looked stunned for an instant. He threw a match into the charcoal and it coughed into flames. He squirted more starter fluid into the orange flames and they shot higher. "How about another drink? You could use a refill to take some of that edge off," he said.

"Ok," Paul said. His head felt light again, almost as if it weren't attached to his body. Perhaps it had been the heat, combined with the booze, that made him so testy. Whatever it was, he liked it. It was becoming easier and easier to say what was on his mind. He was less intimidated. Donny was just a man, like himself, vulnerable as anybody to sharp, decisive criticism. He might, if the conditions presented themselves, confront the fucker today.

□   □

Owen Brown negotiated the turn into McElvay's Fish Camp widely; the boat he towed bounced awkwardly behind him. He was still not used to the inconvenience of having only one eye. Although it was not a permanent condition, it was one giant pain in the ass. He stopped the yellow Ford van on the concrete pad by the gas pumps and swung out of the driver's seat.

He went inside, and from McElvay's wife, a round-faced woman who always wore a bloody apron wrapped around her midriff, and who always smelled as though she had just finished cleaning fish, he bought a quart of Quaker State outboard motor oil. "Look like you lost the battle, boy," she drawled.

Owen smiled weakly and took his change. He had had so much of that grit humor lately that he thought he was going to scream. The dark cinder block inside of McElvay's trapped the cool moisture. An aerator in the live-bait well murmured incessantly, and the sour smell of fish bubbled throughout the room. Behind Mrs. Mac, next to a forest of cane poles, stood the little Negro boy who worked for them. He giggled at Mrs. Mac's remark. Owen said, "Come on out to the pumps."

Owen climbed in the back of the boat. The Negro boy was wearing shorts; his feet and shins were powdered white from the parking lot dust. He cranked the handle on the pump and held it up to Owen, who carefully mixed the gas and oil. When he was finished, he handed the hose down.

21

He jerked his head as if to flick a lock of hair out of his eye, but then he realized it was the bandage and not his hair at all.

"What happen choo?" the boy asked. "What Miz Mac say?"

"No battle."

"What then?"

"A fight," Owen said.

"Joo lose?" he giggled, showing his purple gums. "Guess you did. Even if you winned, you lose."

Everyone was getting on his case, and nobody, not a single soul, knew what he had been through. He wanted to pick up the paddle and chase Mrs. Mac's boy all over the lot and show him exactly who lost. His eye still felt like he had a handful of sand in it, and he remembered vividly the horror of the knife-sharp talons only inches from his face before he blacked out. Once, in the hospital, he had awakened screaming, and when his nurse had come in, she had found him with the dressing torn from his eye.

"Was you out fishin' on the lake yesterday?" the Negro boy asked.

"Why? Did you see me?"

"Nope," the boy said. He pinched his copper face into a raisin as he looked up into the sun, and at Owen standing there in the boat. "But I see one of the sure signs of it."

"What do you mean?"

"You fixin' to take a couple of steps back into the end of you life."

Owen turned and saw a small black moccasin curled in a puddle of water under one of the seats. "Shit," he yelled as he hopped over the side. He landed half on the wheel-well and half on the ground, twisting his ankle. "That wasn't funny, you sonofabitch."

"Was to me," the boy said. "I wasn't in the boat."

When he had been fishing that morning, it must have dropped out of one of the cypress trees that rimmed the lake.

He opened the back of his van and took out his rifle. He propped it beside the van, and picked up one of the paddles. He leaned over the side, and with the flat end, worked the paddle so that he had it underneath the snake. He lifted it quickly and the snake stayed balanced on the end.

"I have it when you done?" the boy asked.

The snake began to slip off the paddle as he walked away from the boat. "You can have it now," Owen said, throwing it at the boy.

"Shiiit," he yelled, and ran. The snake lay stunned where it landed.

Owen took his arm out of the sling and picked up his rifle. Living with Crosby, out on the farm, he must have killed a poisonous snake once a week. Corals, moccasins, rattlers. He had even been bitten by a small moccasin. He aimed squarely at the coiled snake, its black back now a dusty white like the Negro boy's legs, and squeezed off a shot. It echoed over the lake and back. He missed. The snake began to unwind and crawl slowly away. Owen fired another shot. Mrs. McElvay came running out. "What's goin' on out here?" she yelled. She had a bloody knife in her hand. She looked to where Owen was pointing the rifle, then went back inside. From behind the cooler, the black boy hollered, "Kill it, motherfuckah, kill it."

Owen walked closer. He would not be able to hit it from any distance with one eye. The doctors had told him that with his temporary loss of binocular vision, he would have trouble doing even the simplest things. Like killing a snake? He practically put the barrel to the snake's head, and fired his final shot. The snake jumped in the air from the impact. "Shiiit," Owen heard again. The black boy came out from behind the ICE cooler. "You a motherfuckah," he said.

Owen balled up a five-dollar bill for the gas and threw it at the boy. "There's your snake," he said. "Take him home with you."

Driving out to Donny's cabin along Highway 20, a two-lane obstacle course riddled with construction equipment, flashing amber lights and detours, he felt shitty. That kid hadn't done anything to him. He was just dumping on him like he had been dumped on. He was the weakest thing around at the time. Life was like that. Pecking orders, with the weakest catching most of the flak.

And he had still not gotten to where he could kill a snake and not feel bad. Or anything for that matter. He hated killing fish the most. You had to hold them in your hands to do it, and you felt the life die convulsively right there. The feeling stayed with you, like smoking too much dope or doing too much speed, till your system could dilute it. He could still see that snake, its head shredded by the bullet, the skin, like a piece of torn cloth, barely holding it on. When he drove away, its tail was twitching.

That time he had been bitten by the moccasin, he went berserk with panic. Though it was a gray dusk, his vision went crimson. Everything was a shade of red. He thought, Christ, not now, not me. I haven't done enough. He felt the burning sting of the bite at his instep, felt it start into his blood. He ached with fear. Death was supposed to follow some triumph in life. This was bullshit. It could not be random. Why not a head-on collision with a carload of deaf-mutes? Why didn't it come when you were ready for it? Ah, there's the rub; it would not come if you were ready for it.

He had given that little spade something to think about, though. He had never seen anybody move as quickly as Mrs. Mac's boy moved.

Owen carefully pulled to the side of the road by Prairie Creek. It had been part of the flood plain once, but when the water level dropped, all the vegetation died off, leaving only a handful of dried-out cypress shells. Ospreys built their nests in the tops of the dead trees, and this was the time of year when they began coming from their winter migration. He took a pair of binoculars from his glove compartment and watched them from the driver's seat of the van. He took a joint from the ashtray and lit it. It seemed like this was the only way he could unwind now. Somewhere along the line, his mainspring had queered and he had found pot to help it along. The sweet smell of smoke filled the compartment like incense.

In the top of one of the trees, dead and stripped gray of its bark, a pair of ospreys tended something. One of them beat its wings several times, then effortlessly lifted from the nest and flew overhead toward the creek.

Owen followed him with the glasses. He was always amazed at the beauty of flight; not so much in the lesser birds that fluttered on stubby wings and had to undulate in the air to stay up. His awe was inspired by the flight of birds of prey; the strong stroking of long wings, the way they coasted on thermals, sensing a rise, probably seeing it. Shit, he thought, I want to be reborn as that.

He pulled back out on the highway, the boat bouncing behind him. He could feel the weight shift through the chassis of the van, into the steering wheel itself. The motor strained. A car blew its horn, and he looked quickly in the sideview mirror; it was coming on fast. He stuck out his arm, and waved it past, then slid it back in the sling.

Paul's Day. He was happy Paul got to see something as exciting as he did. As it had stood within the Group, the only eagle Paul ever saw in the wild had been when Owen had taken them all on the Ocklawaha trip. He knew Paul thought his single sighting was a source of embarrassment. The eagle had circled them for nearly ten minutes, and Paul had not been excited about it at all. They could tell it was an eagle from the flight profile, but it never flew close enough for him to appreciate its magnificence. That was the thing about eagles; they would never fly close enough. But Paul was right up there now, with Donny and Crosby, and, he had to admit, with himself. Paul finally had a *real* story to tell. And that's all they seemed ever to do. Gather and tell stories about eagles and get drunk as hell.

Paul had brought Owen into the Group. He had told him once, as they sat in his office, that he was a bright student, and that he might get one hell of a kick out of their meetings. "We're a concerned group of conservationists," he had said. "And we're zeroing in on the problems of the bald eagle as an indicator of what's happening with the rest of our ecosystems." Though it had turned out to be anything but that.

Paul had been trying so hard those days, playing surrogate father with him. He had been devastated to find out that Owen had left home at sixteen, and that he hadn't seen his family since. He said Owen intrigued him. At first, he didn't mind. But soon Paul was bird-dogging him everywhere he went, and the surrogate shit turned into a pain in the ass. Paul even started to ask him personal things, things he had no right to know, and he had said, "Goddamnit, Paul, stop trying to be my father." He had been furious. But later, when he had calmed down, he explained that he would end up hating Paul if he didn't stop. All he wanted was to be his friend. After that, Owen thought, they had been like brothers. It was an improvement anyway.

Owen checked the boat swaying easily behind him. Exhaust rising from the engine between the seats replaced the sweet smell of the pot, and it was giving him a headache. The air was warm and he turned the wing vent all the way in, letting the wind whip his hair.

He had a feeling that Paul's wife was at the root of this new tension in the Group. Even the old man, Crosby, had mentioned something to him. He had no idea how Paul had managed to land her. What a cunt. He wanted her so badly every time he saw her that he finally understood the compulsion to rape. She had a way of walking, strutting, that was unnatural, as though she harnessed the vitality of several women. When she turned those green eyes on you, you thought you were the only person in the world she wanted to talk to. Next to Paul, whose thin gaunt frame and darkening complexion seemed to be falling apart under God knows what pressure, she was a stark contrast.

Owen relit the roach and took another couple of hits, then tossed it out the window. He had smoked with Paul several times in his office at the university. That had been one of his biggest kicks, turning on his teacher. What *were* things coming to? He wondered if Donny, who was younger, didn't also take to the weed. Paul had wanted to be cool. He could see it in the way he held the joint, the way he didn't hold in the smoke. Donny probably smoked behind everybody's back, ever conscious of the proper political profile. Yes, he thought, Donny was like that. Perhaps he would take Paul aside before he spun his yarn for the Group and get him wasted. He had done that once, before his Tennyson class, and they had both marveled at how much more lucid he had been.

☐   ☐

Paul watched a blackened ash work its way up the column of heat given off by the glowing coals, an imaginary eagle coasting the thermals. His mouth felt stuffed with cotton, and there was an unexplainable sweet taste in the back of his throat. Maybe change to beer now, he thought. The crunch of tires on the driveway interrupted the unbearable stillness of the afternoon. He felt like a prisoner. When he saw the yellow van round the final bend, he waved. He

27

decided that he would have no more at all to drink, and that he was happy the kid had showed up.

Donny came out the side door. He yelled directions to Owen, who made several miscalculations in backing the van around. "Do it till you get it right," Donny yelled to him. "I don't have all goddamned day," Owen shot back. Finally he had the van backed around the trees that dotted Donny's yard, and the trailer in the water. He came around behind and uncranked the boat. When it floated free, he waded the bow around till it nuzzled the dock and he tied it up.

As he came out of the water, Donny clapped him on the back and said, "How ya doing, Owen?"

"Touch and go."

Paul walked drunkenly toward them. The thick sand had his feet baffled.

"You look great," Paul slurred. "Where's Crosby?"

"Great-looking bandage," Donny said. "Great."

"He'll be along."

"Fuck you," Paul said.

"Huh?" Owen said.

"Not you. Him."

"Crosby said he wouldn't ride in my van since I nearly took the side of his porch off. Said I was crazy to drive it one-handed, and towing a boat at the same time. Said he valued his life a heap more than that, what he has left of it, and that he'd be here when he got here." Owen turned from Donny to Paul. "And haven't you had enough to drink?"

"Is it true what the professor says?" Donny asked.

"Sure. I saw it. With my own eye." They laughed, but it did not take any of the edges off.

"That wouldn't do a hell of a lot in a court of law. Great-looking boat you got there."

"I know," Owen said. "Nice, ain't it?"

"Ain't it?" Paul mimicked.

It was a pale blue and white Glassmaster, with a small cushioned deck, and a 75-horsepower Evinrude.

"What'll she do?" Donny asked. His *thing* had given him notoriety throughout Putnam County. He was the speedball attorney with the midnight blue MG. Owen had told him once that it was just another part of his colossal impatience with the world. Ever since he had described the boat to him, Donny had been after him to bring it out to the lake so that he could put it through its paces. "How fast'll she go?"

"Don't know," Owen said. "I thought I'd leave that to you."

"Who's gonna ski first, then?"

"That's stupid," Paul said. "Owen can't ski because of his arm. And Crosby isn't here." Paul paused as though he had just figured something out, "And besides, he's old enough to be your grandfather."

Paul looked for something weak in Donny's eyes, but they reflected like mirrors. This stuff kept blurting out. He couldn't control it. Was this madness? If all this turned up wrong, he'd be in one hell of a bind with Donny. It was all stupid. But there was the smell. And he did bring them together for dinner. He *was* responsible for setting this thing in motion, and he would have to be the one to end it. What ate at him was watching Donny's lips as he spoke, and imagining them on Lorene's taut breasts. Or his hands, with those manicured nails, running over her stomach. Or worse.

"Got a point, Paul. Let's have another drink, then you and I'll go."

Inside, Donny asked Owen if he would help Tuesday by driving voters to the polls.

"All right," he said. "But if you win, I'll expect some form of gratuity. A fat political plum."

"Not funny," Donny said.

"Spare me," Paul said.

"Spare you what?"

Owen said, "Ten years from now, they'll have the shit corrupted out of you." He popped open a beer, and took a swallow. "You'll be so thick with them, flies'll swarm wherever you go. I'll be saying, 'I knew him when . . .'"

"Eat it," Donny said. It was arrogance for Owen to tread that way into his territory. He did not take his career lightly, and he did not consider it cute for Owen to lecture him on the dangers of corruption in times like these, no matter how flippantly.

He had been out of law school for nearly five years, and he had modestly assessed his own political development as meteoric. Working for the public defender's office for the first two years had given him invaluable trial experience, even though he nearly starved. It was all calculated to one end and he didn't need Owen rubbing his nose in political shit.

"Let's hit the water," Donny told Paul.

"I want to spin around the lake first and look it over."

"There's no gators," Donny taunted him.

Paul said flatly, "I had a friend that skied into a stump once because he was careless. Nearly took his leg off."

"You needn't worry so much."

Paul and Donny walked out of the house together, across the short yard, sparse with slash pines and turkey oaks, to the dock where they both climbed into the boat.

Owen sat back at Donny's desk sipping a beer, and watched them. He pulled a joint from his pocket and lit it. These two had made a knot in his belly with their snapping at each other. There was something coming to a head with this nit-shit, and he wished that he hadn't come. It just wasn't going to be his day. First the fisherwoman, then the spade, now these two. He decided to see if he could smoke exactly half and get sufficiently loaded before they got back.

Donny started the engine. The noise echoed around the

lake. He backed out slowly. Paul stood beside him, holding on to the Plexiglas windshield. Donny gunned the engine, tossing Paul back into the seat. The bow raised, and the boat made a sharply delineated white wake, like a rip, on the smooth brown surface of the water.

"Slow it down," Paul yelled. "Are you crazy?"

Donny pushed the throttle forward, and the nose settled comfortably. The engine dropped from a roar to a gentle idle and the wake caught up to them from behind.

"Don't be such an old lady," Donny said.

"Drive around the edges."

Paul watched Donny's wide shoulders underneath his terrycloth beach jacket work the wheel. He made a large arc around the banks. Little spasms rippled his shoulders and Paul knew he was just dying to open the throttle full. He felt strong containing him this way. Donny's hair caught in a breeze and lifted stiffly. It had not been so much what he had done with her, Paul thought, but what *she* had done with him.

"You go in for those gossip magazines?" Paul said to Donny's back. "I mean that one in particular: *People in the News.*" His voice trembled slightly on the word *News,* but over the sound of the engine, he was sure Donny didn't detect it.

Donny did not turn. "Can't stand that muck."

"What's it doing on your coffee table then?" Lorene had told him once that it was like the gossip page of the Sunday Magazine, only better because there was nothing else in the magazine but gossip. Paul wanted to win a skirmish right now. He needed a small one to give him something firm to stand on later.

Without a flinch, Donny said, "I keep it there for my clients. Sometimes I do business at the house."

"You said you *never* do business at the house. That's what your office is for."

"Sometimes I do. What's the big deal about a goddamned gossip magazine?" He turned and caught Paul's eyes when he said gossip magazine. Paul thought somehow the whole thing had gotten turned around on him.

When they got to the dock, Paul stormed into the house, went into the back bedroom and changed into his swim suit. When he came out, Owen asked him, "You all right? You're acting pretty raggedy."

Paul paced the porch. "Fine. I'm fine. I'm just getting a little tired of the superior attitude that sonofabitch has all the time." He felt shaky, skitterish. He wanted to relax but he couldn't sit still.

"Maybe you ought to pass up skiing for today."

"I said I'm all right," he snapped.

Donny came in and pulled his trunks from where they hung on a nail by the fishing rods.

"Where's the equipment?" Paul asked Owen.

Owen took a long pull on his beer, finishing it, and let out a roar of a belch. "Out in the back of the van. Can I take another beer, Donny?"

"Sure." Donny slipped off his trousers and pulled on the white suit that matched his beach jacket.

"Well, I'm going to get wet," Paul said. He turned to Donny. "You get the stuff." He walked out the door, letting it swing closed behind him with a crack. When he got to the water and saw how clear the edges were, he thought: that sonofabitch doesn't deserve to live here. A small brim, silver in the sun, darted away as he stirred the cool water with his foot. Finally, he rubbed his chest furiously with both hands, trying to pull up some warmth, and ran out till he could raise his knees no higher. Then he gave a yell, which sounded somewhat like a scream echoing across the lake, and dove in.

As he surfaced, he gulped for air. The coldness had taken his breath. There was still a winter chill to the water. And he was still a little drunk from the Scotch. Maybe a lot drunk. He would take Owen aside to see if he had anything to smoke. Like a nervine, it had a calming effect on him. He treaded water and watched the terns on the far side of the lake, small and white with their funny black masks, dip to the water and steal minnows, then fly away. When he heard the porch door slam, he jerked around. Donny came bounding from the house and headed for the van.

Donny had decided that he would not let Paul get to him. He had the barbecue planned, and there was more than enough booze in the house to dilute the most abrasive of personalities, which, he thought, Paul was fast becoming. Sometime after Tuesday, when it was all over, he would deal with Paul.

Donny opened the back of the van, and next to a small caliber rifle, found the equipment Owen had rented. The nylon ski rope was coiled neatly beside the skis, which had crossed themselves. He carried them to the boat, tied the rope to the cleats, and threw the belt and skis in the back.

He started the engine and revved it. The thick smell of gasoline and oil erupted in bubbles from the prop. There was something about the speed with which this boat's fiber glass hull planed over the water that he liked. Loved. He edged the boat past Paul, left the controls, and carefully began letting out the rope so it wouldn't foul the prop.

"I'm going to make another pass or two," he yelled to Paul. He threw the belt to him, then each of the skis. They slid quickly over the water, then bobbed in the ripples given off by the engine.

Paul swam to them. He pulled the styrofoam belt around his waist and buckled it. Immediately, it slid up under his armpits. Donny gunned the engine and Paul watched the bow rise completely out of the water. He seemed to be going faster than the boat was capable of going. That son-ofabitch better not pull me like that. He held his face underwater and, in the blur, worked his feet awkwardly into the skis. When he raised his head, he saw that the hull of the boat had finally settled, and Donny was coming straight at him. Fast. The fucker's crazy.

Donny nosed the boat away, rounded the cove where his house sat, made another sweep around the lake, and began to close his circles until he was about fifty feet from Paul.

"Great boat," he yelled, alternately gunning and slowing the engine, like a hot-rodder catching rubber.

"If you think you're going to pull me like that, you're crazy."

"For Christ's sake," Donny said, "you're getting worse than the old man. Why don't you swim back to the dock, and I'll take you out on ladies' night."

"Fuck you."

He continued to circle as Paul adjusted his skis. He waved to Owen standing at the porch door and raised the bow. Owen raised his middle finger in salute. He made two larger passes, then straightened the boat just past where Paul floated. "You ready?"

Paul did not hear Donny. His attention was distracted to the rope which had somehow entangled his waist. The skis turned tip down, and crossed as he tried to free himself. It took a lot of effort for him to raise them. He raised a hand and called back, "Wait. I think I'm caught." His arms were heavy as logs from treading water and his head whirled now from the exertion. He pulled at the rope but was not having much success with it. He wished that he had not had so much to drink.

The boat bobbed in rhythm to the engine's two-stroke cadence. A puff of blue smoke, smelling thickly of oil, wafted away from the water. Donny waved back to him, turned and gunned the engine.

Paul felt an instant of slackness, then the nylon rope cut into his sides. It spun him toward shore, like a top. He thought he had come free, but the rope had merely slipped to his ankle, and then it jerked him. In that moment of sheer panic, he saw Owen come down one step from the porch. Their eyes locked; Owen's mouth was a gaping hole against his bandaged face.

The boat accelerated, pulling him deeper. The skis came off instantly. One of them grazed his head. He was drawn down into colder water. The loud and endless acceleration of bubbles deafened him. He clamped his mouth tightly shut. With his arms, he clawed feverishly against the water. Bubbles streaked the length of his body, seeming almost solid. The only thing solid. He wanted to gulp them in his mouth. He tried pushing against them. From the very center of his groin, he felt a burning liquid begin to erupt. When it had finally coursed up through his chest, he thought his heart exploded, and he let out the scream that waited in his throat.

CHAPTER

As DONNY ACCELERATED, THE FRONT OF THE BOAT LIFTED, then jerked as if it had hit a stump. It lifted higher, and the engine seemed to drag. He became worried that he had screwed something up. He didn't need Owen on his back today too. A rabid husband was enough for anybody. Crosby would be there soon and they could get on with their meeting and the barbecue. He wanted to be done with the whole crew of them right now. He would pass up skiing for another time.

He turned and looked behind. Paul. He did not see him. What kind of joke was this? He pulled the throttle back full, trying to remedy the kink by going faster. It had always worked with his car. Worked or broke altogether. The nose lifted higher. He looked behind again and saw nothing, yet the engine was dragging more. He decided that Paul could go screw for his skiing.

36

As he rounded the inlet and pressed for the house, he saw Owen running out to the end of the dock. Owen started jumping up and down, waving his arms frantically; his sling danced uselessly from his neck. Shit, he thought, he hoped he hadn't seen him hit that stump.

When he got closer, Owen dropped his arms. He slowed the engine; the nose settled finally and comfortably in the water. The boat bobbed above a white line of backwash. Donny pulled parallel to the dock. He was just about to ask where the hell that asshole Paul had gone to, when Owen dove in and swam out behind the boat.

He turned to see Owen tugging at the ski line. Paul's pink and red rounded back broke the surface of the water and floated listlessly, face down. His dark hair was a tangle against the darker water. His left arm twisted unnaturally over his back so that his hand rested, palm upward, on his rump.

"Jesus Christ," Donny screamed. He stood there frozen for an eternity. Owen swam weakly to the dock, alternately spitting water and gasping for air. Then Donny reached over the stern and helped Owen drag the line in.

"I didn't know it," Donny said. His voice cracked. "Oh, Jesus, help me, Owen. Is he dead?"

He crossed to the dock and they lifted Paul's body out of the water. The rope had slipped down to his ankle and tightened. His toes looked like an enlarged cluster of purple grapes, and not at all part of his pale body. His face had contorted into a grimace.

Owen blew air into Paul's mouth. His chest rose and fell, but would not start of its own. His lips were cold as snow, felt plastic. He reeked of alcohol.

"Is he dead?" Donny kept asking.

Finally, Owen straightened from where he knelt. "I think so. Why didn't you look behind you? Didn't you hear me yelling that you were dragging him?"

"Shit. Shit. I didn't hear anything. The goddamned engine

was so loud." As Owen stood up, Donny grabbed him by the shoulder. His fingers sunk deep to the bone. Owen felt like he had been speared again by those talons. At that moment, he saw the bird attacking, saw it in the wild green eyes and the sharp brow and a shiver racked his body. "Let go of me," he shouted, jerking away.

"It was a goddamned accident." Donny's voice strained. His face was scarlet. Donny began pacing in front of Paul. His insides roiled dark and fast in a frenzy of recriminations. "What am I gonna do? Jesus Christ, what am I gonna do?"

Owen knelt again to examine Paul. It was all too unreal. A puddle of water spread out from him like an aura. His wet skin felt cold and snakelike. When he touched him now, his hand recoiled uncontrollably. Paul's body was covered with red welts, and looked as though it had bounced along the bottom, perhaps hitting against those stumps that he so desperately feared. He had a knot at the base of his skull the size of an orange. The drowning hadn't killed him. It was the blow to the head. Why hadn't Donny felt the boat jerking under his hands? Or stopped to see why the bow had risen so ungodly high out of the water? At the speed he was going, he should have felt something.

"You should have felt it," Owen said. "You should have known."

"What do you mean?" Donny snapped before he had finished.

"Nothing. Just that I would have known."

"Well, I didn't." Donny's face changed suddenly, as if it was darkened by an overhead cloud. The veins in his forehead pulsed, then faded.

Donny jumped back down into the boat and turned off the engine. He sat there a moment, absorbed in the silence that curtained the lake. It was as though the quiet had somehow imposed an order, a rationality to the situation. He had been so preoccupied with himself, and with taunting Paul, that he hadn't been thinking straight. He should have felt it, like Owen said. God, why had this happened? What makes things turn out this way? Who says it's *your* turn now to fuck up? Make it good.

He started the engine again, and turned away from the dock.

Owen shouted, "Where are you going?"

In the center of the lake, he shut the engine down and hung over the side to retrieve the skis. When he came back in, he pulled in the rope and coiled it in the back of the boat. Then he jumped to the dock. "Listen," he said, "we can't act on this now. I mean, no police."

"What?"

"You heard me. No police."

"Bullshit. You killed him. You have to report it."

"It was an accident, goddamnit." He moved closer to Owen. His whole face flared, transformed demonically.

"I didn't mean it to sound like that," Owen said. "I know it was an accident. I saw it, but we have to report it."

"He's dead and there's nothing we can do about it. Smell my breath," Donny said. "I'd never pass a Breathalyzer test." He was frantic now. He bent to Paul and pinched his flaccid cheeks so that his mouth popped open like a fish. "Smell his. Reporting it won't serve anybody. Please, Owen, let's think this out a minute." His voice was supplicant, his hands began to flutter uncontrollably about his face. He would not look at Paul. "It'll ruin everything. My life. I . . . I can't."

"If you don't call the cops, I will. We could get in all kinds of trouble . . ."

Donny did a double take as Owen began to walk toward the cabin. "It'll ruin my life," he said again, but there was no pleading in his voice now. There was a sharp edge to it; it bordered on a bellow. "What makes you so goddamned righteous? You can't throw my life away with a fucking phone call!" He had jumped in front of Owen in an instant, cutting off his exit. He pushed him back. Owen stumbled over Paul's leg and Donny was on top of him before he hit the dock.

"Craz . . ."

Donny punched at Owen's face. His knuckles grazed the side of his head.

"My eye," Owen yelled.

"It was a goddamned accident," Donny screamed. He had worked his knees up over Owen's arms and sat practically on, his neck. His scarlet throat swelled and pumped like a chameleon's.

"Crazy shit. Get off."

"Ruin . . . my . . . life." Each word was punctuated with a wild punch. He ripped the soggy gauze dressing from Owen's eye. "Crazy? I'll poke your motherfucking eye out."

"Don't hit it, don't hit it." Owen jerked his head back and forth, avoiding Donny's fist. His entire being was in his neck, stretching, twisting.

Donny grabbed a fistful of hair, and began banging Owen's head against the dock. Every tension he had ever had—from the campaign, from tomorrow's trial, from the sheer self-destructiveness of his relationship with Paul's wife—pulsed through him and out his arms in some magnificent power. *This was madness,* a voice inside him screamed. He was more frightened of this than of the consequences of Paul's death because he was for the first time outside himself, outside his own control. He could see what he was doing, see himself on top of Owen, on top of Paul, and he could not stop.

"All right. All right," Owen said. "Anything." Donny's face had contorted itself into an obscene drooling mask. His eyes bulged. The muscles in his neck twined spasmodically. Owen felt as if his brain had come loose. The blood drummed inside his head from a point at the base of his skull. It pushed at his eyes, his nostrils, every opening of his

40

face till he thought the top of his head would explode right there and spill out on the dock.

Donny rolled off him. First Owen started to cry, then Donny. It was the only sound on the lake, great heaving sobs. Owen's leg was still pinned across Paul's chest. He was so scared he thought he was going to die. His mind wouldn't work at all. A chill wracked him; his skin tingled and he was afraid that he was going into shock. He could feel every vein and artery inside him dilate and the blood slow as his heart rocked inside his chest. The beating reverberated against the dock, till it expanded outside his body. He wanted to jump up and catch it, but all he could do was surrender.

Slowly, Donny got up. "Help me," he said. He was still sobbing. A line of mucus ran from his nose like a river. He lifted Paul under his shoulders and began to drag him from the dock. Paul left a trail of water like a slug. "Take his feet."

"I can't."

"Take his feet, goddamnit."

They carried him off the dock and laid him in the sand underneath the raised foundation of the cabin. Owen had never lifted anything so heavy in his life. He had carried a girl who had fainted once, but limp as she was, there was still a lightness to her body. Paul was heavier than a sack of wet concrete.

Donny covered Paul with a tarp. "Wait here," he said. He ran in the house, then out the front door. Owen heard the sputtering of Paul's Volkswagen, heard Donny grind the gears, and heard it finally drive away. He felt like he was stuck in a dream, chained to that tarp-covered lump beside him. His own limbs felt abnormally heavy, like he had over-dosed on barbiturates; his eye ached with a single, pointed pain. He did not know how long Donny had been gone.

First he heard his feet crunching the brittle oak leaves, then his voice. "Get in the house and gather his clothes."

"What are you going to do?"

Donny struggled to lift Paul's body over his shoulder. He looked straight through Owen. "Move it," he said. Then, "Your eye is oozing, why don't you fix it."

Owen went inside. He went to the window in the back bedroom to see what Donny was doing. He would jump in the van and haul ass as soon as that crazy motherfucker positioned himself in such a way so he could escape. When he pulled up the shades, though, he saw Donny at the back of *his* van, with the door open.

"What the fuck are you doing?" he yelled.

Donny dumped Paul from his shoulder into the van and reeled around, but he did not answer.

Paul's clothes were thrown on the bed. Owen studied them for an instant. He felt he didn't belong there; he didn't need to see this. It was obvious that Paul had been weirded out. His trousers were balled at one end of the bed, his shirt hung on one of the bedposts, a sleeve turned inside out. His socks and underwear lay on the floor right where he must have stepped out of them. It reminded him of a picture he had seen once of Gandhi's possessions, meager and neatly stacked together with obvious attention to final details. And Paul, as in so many nightmares Owen had about himself, got snuffed in the middle of everything. It was the coarsest, most unheroic end a person could have. It was over for him and all the untidy ends would have to be cleaned up by someone else, hands insensitive to the delicacies of his life. Why wasn't his wife here? She should be doing this. She should be seeing his vulnerabilities strewn across this room.

He gathered Paul's shirt and pants. Coins jingled in the pockets. He counted the change. Fifty-two cents. Two dollar bills. When he bent to pick up his tennis shoes he realized that the whole room had been permeated with their sour odor, the smells of feet and rubber. As bad as it was, it smelled good to him. It was the last smell of Paul he would ever have. That's a hell of an epitaph. Sour feet. At once he thought he would like to save it in a jar. Savor it. Concrete proof of Paul's existence. He would take it to the cops and tell them: this is what death smells like, or better, Paul's wife. Your husband's final smell. Rubber. Rubbish.

"Owen," Donny called. His voice drifted calmly now across the yard. Owen was more afraid of Donny than he had ever been of anything. He could still see Paul's eyes, the utter and startled disbelief in what was happening as he went under. They had locked together in that instant, and he had felt his own life pulled from him. And there was Donny, his back turned, oblivious, hurtling across the water.

"Owen," he heard again. The voice sounded planned, the voice of a parent calling his kid in from a game of pickup softball.

Finally, Donny said, "Goddamnit, Owen," loud as a clap of thunder. Owen jumped as if he had been struck. From where he stood by the bed, he saw Donny's face pushed into the darkened screen. His nose was flattened against it, horrifying. "Get your ass out here."

Owen bundled the clothes. Outside, he handed them to Donny, who threw them in the back of the van and closed the door. "After Tuesday, I'll straighten everything out. There won't be any repercussions."

"Straighten out? You just killed Paul. How the hell are you going to straighten that out?"

"I don't know yet. I need time though. Just a little time."

Owen realized Donny's coolness was thinly held together by some external force. Inside, it seemed as though a volcano seethed, as if he could stay together only if he kept moving. He held his eyes unnaturally wide, and his shoulders ticked rhythmically, like a metronome. "Get in," Donny said.

Owen took out a roll of gauze from the glove compartment and some tape. He cut strips of tape and laid them across his legs. He turned the mirror to watch as he placed the gauze over his reopened eye. The skin had gathered, and there was a small ulcerated opening that oozed slightly. He saw the tarp-covered lump behind him on the floor. He did not know if the van had quickly filled with the smell of those tennis shoes, or if the smell was still in his nose from the house. He worried that he would never be freed from that smell.

Donny unhitched the boat trailer from the back of the van and pushed it to the side of the cabin. Then he got in the van and backed it out the driveway onto Blanding Road.

"Jesus Christ, I'm not a bad man," Donny said. "You understand that." He did not look at Owen. His chest was alive with trembling; his voice was weak for the first time. This was no way to address the jury, Owen thought. "It was an accident that Paul's life had to end," he continued, "but going to the cops would be throwing mine away."

"I don't understand any of this," Owen said. One eye burned, the other teared.

He wanted to get to a doctor. He had always believed that the steps you took when confronted with death were simple, laid out for you by the system. You just called the appropriate authority. But Donny *was* the system. And this bizarre reality was unraveling in dangerous ways.

He stared blankly out the window. He could not keep his eye focused. He knew he was more the prisoner of this lunatic than responsible for what had happened, and yet fear held him fastened to the seat as tightly as if he had been tied there. He felt utterly helpless. The same kind of helplessness he felt while careening madly through the heavens with three hundred people in a jumbo jet. There was just no way to get off these rides. He had been on them before, holding his fear in check, knowing all it would take was something sudden and he'd pee in his pants, or worse.

Donny followed Blanding Road till he came to the first paved road in Putnam Hall, where the railroad tracks crossed. He turned on Milledge and followed the tracks through town.

"I'm not a bad man," Donny kept repeating. It was like a mantra to him now. "I'm not a bad man." It would keep his head from whirling away, from flying off into space. Owen had to believe it; he had to believe it himself. These were mitigating circumstances in the truest sense. No longer just legal jargon to throw around a courtroom. It is here; it is now; it is real. God save the law and God save me.

When Donny passed the BAY station, he blew the horn reflexively. Owen started in the seat beside him. The attendant waved. Habit. His hand had honked before he knew what he was doing. That kind of carelessness could cost me, Donny thought. If that kid only knew there was a corpse in the back, he'd shit. *A corpse*. The word rocked his brain. Paul, goddamnit. Don't lose sight of that. Paul, he said to himself. A man. A jellyfish, a spineless . . . A man.

White clapboard houses fronted the railroad tracks. They had screened porches cast in deep shadows. Donny marked each one, looking for something different about their yards or the way the hedges were clipped. The paint on some of them was peeling and they looked a mottled gray, not at all unlike the color of an immature great blue heron. In the old days, the days when Crosby first came, the houses would have been inhabited by Yankees who'd taken the train down from up north to step out right at their front doors. Then the freezes came and drove them farther south. They left so fast, Crosby had told him, that they didn't even bother to clear their dinner plates from the table.

Then squatters came and took over their houses and he

was looking at their descendants now, swaying lazily on the rusty-chained porch swings, their dishes stacked neatly on their drainboards, their dinners comfortably settling in their bellies. They were watching him too, as he bounced slowly through the chuckholes of their poorly paved street. Some of them even waved.

When they passed the sheriff's office, not much bigger than a cinder-block shed tucked into the ominous tendrils of two neatly spaced live oaks, Owen contemplated jumping. A moment of utter despair had wedged itself into his packed head and he weighed the impact of the jump against the movement of the van. He saw himself splayed and bouncing uncontrollably on the orange clay of the shoulder, a plume of dust arcing steadily behind him.

It did not occur to Owen where the hell Donny was going, nor did it occur to him to ask. But when Donny turned the van into the dirt side road that led to the Kaolin Industries mines, the skin prickled at the back of his neck.

□   □

For the past twenty years, since a chemical company from Mississippi discovered the priceless clay buried underneath the worthless sandhills community, the mines had been worked, and even at night you could hear the incessant grumble of conveyor belts hauling out tons of Kaolin. It was drawn from the earth by great burrowing machines, leaving deep gorges like some prehistoric cave community. The holes trailed so far underground, it was rumored that cave explorers from the university had gone in, and never come out.

A few scraggly turkey oaks remained on the horizon, bare and still dormant from winter. They had not yet turned the first high green of spring. The sand hills were powdered white, and in the waning afternoon light they glistened like snowbanks. Storage tanks lined the rusted, corrugated aluminum building. Huge inverted cones of clay tailings, like giant anthills, waited for the morning to be moved into the parked Eastern Seaboard sidecars on the tracks. The machines looked frozen in the middle of their last action.

The yellow van pulled in the gate, bounced slowly over the cattle grating, then drove to a remote corner of the yard. Donny backed around to the edge of one of the ravines and shut down the engine. He jumped out, then slung open the rear door. "I'll handle this myself."

Owen did not know if he could talk or not. He felt his mind drawing in on itself, each wrinkle of his brain compressing. He looked straight out the front window at the desolate yard, the funnel stack blackened and smokeless. Donny grunted as he lifted. From the side window, he watched Donny, with the tarp-covered mass slung over his shoulder, make his way carefully over the side of the crevice and down to where one of the cullers was poised. The strength of a madman.

Owen felt he was going crazy. There was a sense of rightness to what was going on. He had never believed anything that had to do with *systems,* and here it was thrown back on him like a giant and overwhelming backfire. Natural justice. He probably would have done the same thing if he had had anything to lose. But he didn't. He knew about that one point in time, where, if you stepped across an imaginary line, transgressed law, you became the irretrievable. It was something he held no respect for. And someone like Donny didn't have the makeup to withstand the recriminations that came with it. It would have to be answered in everything he ever did; it would linger forever.

Donny's head cleared the sharp white line of the top of the ravine. The tarp was thrown over his shoulder and he headed for the van at a dead run. He threw the tarp in and gathered Paul's clothes, then just as quickly disappeared again.

Owen had felt trapped and helpless in the van. Just standing outside and filling his lungs with fresh air was a relief. It was like breaking the surface after a long dive. He gave Donny enough time to go over the side and he followed.

He crouched in a crevice eroded in the clay bank from years of rain and watched Donny pull Paul's bathing suit off. He rolled it in a ball and shoved it in his pocket. Donny's hands worked feverishly, first drawing Paul's limp arm through the shirt sleeve. He dusted his back as he rolled him over and forced his other arm through. He rolled him back and wiped his chest clean of claydust and buttoned the shirt. Then, with the same care and attention to detail, he pulled on Paul's underwear and slacks. Finally he laced on Paul's tennis shoes, having some trouble with the swollen foot. Then he stood him at the edge of the abandoned shaft and watched him crumple forward into the hole. After a second there was a muffled thud.

Owen ran back to the van; his mind reeled wildly. The sonofabitch is trying to make it look like an accident. Like he stumbled drunk into that hole. What about the water in his lungs? What about: how did he get there? What about . . . ? It would never work, and he was going to be dragged down with that crazy sonofabitch. He looked in the ignition for the keys but Donny had removed them.

When Donny got back to the van, Owen was trying to sit in the same pose as when he had left.

"I saw you," Donny said.

"I don't know what you're talking about."

"Don't bullshit me. I wasn't born yesterday. I saw you watching me."

"All right. So what? What are you going to do, kill me?"

"Don't be a smartass." There was a frightening calmness to Donny's voice now. His hands no longer shook. It was as if he had deposited his hysteria along with Paul's body.

"I have to do something about this," Owen said, immediately regretting it.

"Go ahead. But you're an accomplice. I'll sell the world on that. It was your boat, your van, and I'll tell them it was partly your idea. I'll tell them you wanted money to keep from talking and that I refused."

"Nobody in the world would believe that."

"Sheriff Phillips will if I bring you with me."

Donny drove out the gate and headed for his cabin.

Owen had to tell somebody. He couldn't tell that bastard Phillips. He hated his guts. And outside the town, or even outside the county, it was his word against Donny's. Donny had the name, the money, and the tool—his law practice—to save himself. Who the hell would save me, he thought.

"I made a mistake," Donny said, "and God knows I'm sorrier for that than anything I've ever done. I know I'll never sleep. I'll never forget this. How can I? I can feel it already." He turned somber and drove a few minutes in silence. Then he said, "You just forget about reporting anything. We have to try to pick up where we left off."

They found Crosby sitting at Donny's desk. His white head showed above the back of the chair like a half moon turned sideways. When they came upon him, he was looking out over the lake, sipping a beer. The slamming of the door startled him, and he swiveled in the chair to greet them. His eyes had pouches under them, and the eyes themselves were iridescent blue with a mild, liquid look to them. Owen was relieved to see him there; he wanted to fall down and hug him.

"Where the hell have y'all been?" Crosby said. "I've been here nearly an hour."

"Went for a ride," Donny said. "We got tired of waiting for your cantankerous old ass, so I took Owen to see a new nest."

"Productive?"

Donny said, "Think so. One fledgling."

"Where's Paul?"

"Didn't show," Donny said.

Owen felt his balls drop to his knees. Donny looked quickly to him and he had a flash of what Donny had said to him. He imagined himself in jail somewhere, trying to convince some thickheaded cop of the truth of what had happened, trying desperately to get bail posted, and Donny would be out, sucking beer at a bar and getting laid.

"I need a beer," Owen said. He went into the kitchen. Crosby yelled, "I put some in the freezer."

He had to get out of there before Crosby saw he was shaking. His stomach wrenched into knots and he could taste a high sweet nausea in his mouth. He took a Miller from the refrigerator and opened it. It burned coldly into the back of his throat and he vomited in the sink. He felt it rise from his belly, and he thought it would never end, that he would turn inside out.

He could hear Donny telling Crosby, as calmly as if it were the truth, how strange he thought it was that Paul had not shown up today. All of them had known how excited he was to share his new experience of the eagle. Crosby agreed, and remarked how much he knew Paul looked forward to the water too. And on top of all this, he heard Donny pretending he was worried, because Paul hadn't missed a meeting, or so much as been late since the Group began.

Owen went into Donny's bathroom to clean himself. He looked in the mirror. His face was pallid; his lips looked swollen, brownish. On the shelf behind him, he looked for a washcloth to wipe the vomit from his shirt. He smelled awful. He remembered the smell of Paul's tennis shoes in the other room, and how awful they smelled.

There were dozens of bottles: shampoos, rinses, peppermint oil soaps, and cold creams. It looked like a goddamned cosmetics counter, he thought. But there were no washcloths. On the side of the tub, several dried and brittle loofah sponges were stacked. Another hung from the shower fixture. It was shaped like a catcher's mitt.

When Owen came back to the porch, Donny was talking casually about the election. "Be a close one," he said.

"Not as close as you think," Crosby said. "Got my finger on the pulse of it."

Owen saw Donny beaming at Crosby's remark, as though nothing unusual had happened to him.

"Can I put that in the bank?" Donny asked.

"I don't care what you do with it."

"There doesn't seem to be much point in holding the meeting since Paul isn't here," Donny said.

Owen almost shouted, but the shout stuck in his throat and sounded like a belch.

"What's the matter with you, boy?" Crosby said. "Seem a bit sick."

"I gotta get outta here," Owen said. "I'll see you back at the farm." He slammed the door as he walked out of the cabin.

Donny said, "I wonder what's eating him?"

"Needs to get laid."

"How about letting me fix you a real drink?"

"Nope," Crosby said. "That's foolishness for a man my age."

CHAPTER

3

LORENE PICKED FEEBLY AT THE DINNER SHE HAD FIXED FOR both of them. Finally she cleared away the table. She started to wrap the leftovers and put them into the refrigerator, then decided without any reason to throw them away.

The afternoon had been unseasonably warm, and when the sun went down it got cool. She changed out of her halter top and shorts and into a brown floor-length lounging robe. After dark, she sat out on the front steps, occasionally swatting at the mosquitoes. Sometimes they were like this in Key West, but they were never this bad in Dallas. She watched the curve of the Boulevard, and the wash of lights slowly defining themselves into balls of headlamps, then breaking around the bend and away. Sometimes a car or two would drain off the busy road and her stomach would tighten, but none of them pulled into her driveway. The feeling she had been fighting, that same feeling of impending bad news she had gotten about Sara Halfacre that time in her childhood, worked its way into her head. She forgot about being mad and about Paul ruining dinner.

At ten o'clock, she undressed for bed, removed her makeup and washed with Noxzema and Dr. Bronner's, then called Donny.

"How's Paul?" he said.

"What do you mean how's Paul? *Where's* Paul?"

"I don't get it," he said. "When he didn't show up here . . ." He stopped. She knew he was waiting for her to pick it up.

"He didn't show up?" Her voice trailed away. "He left here around noon. He was going straight out to your place."

"Did you tell him anything about us?"

"No. Why?"

"Well, I just thought that might be why he didn't come. You know he's been acting strange lately. Even some of the guys in the Group mentioned it, and so I . . ."

"Stop it," she said. In that moment of silence, she could feel him hanging on his last word, could see that dumb look of consternation he affected to look cute with her. "I'm worried about him. It's not like Paul to do something like this."

"Nonsense. He probably found something out about us and went on a bender." He was so matter-of-fact.

"It's not nonsense," she said. "There are certain things I know. And I know something's wrong."

"Mark my words. He'll probably come staggering home with an enormous hango . . ."

"Thanks for nothing, Donny." She slammed the receiver down. That callous prick. He's enjoying my nervousness, she thought. She went in the bedroom, folded back the covers and lay in bed with the light on. Sara's face, like a dream, kept showing on the back of her eyelids, and she didn't know whether to cry or scream. She was aware of the empty space beside her and the cool sheets. She rolled to her side, turned the thick pillow toward her and edged up beside it. She resisted turning off the light, knowing it would bring something she would not like. Paul had never done anything like this before. He had always been punctual. He had tried to impress that on her. He had said that what you do reflects what you are. It was a matter of respect. Everything he did was a matter of respect. He was big on matters of respect.

She could not sleep. She got up, took three Valium and washed them down with a brandy. She put her robe on again and sat up on the couch. For a while, she tried watching television, but all she got were gray test patterns and an old John Garfield movie.

The most radical thing Paul had ever done in his life was throw his clothes in a knapsack the summer they met, and hitchhike from Gainesville to Key West.

It had been pouring that day, harder than she had ever seen it rain. When she was out on South Beach earlier, sunning herself, she had seen a waterspout. It was about three miles offshore but it split the sky in two like it had been penciled there. It swayed rhythmically and seemed to draw the ocean upward around itself so that when it got closer, it looked like it was raining upside down. She remembered the tornadoes they had in Oklahoma when she was young and it scared her enough to make her ride the bike home.

The sky grayed quickly, and the narrow streets fronted by the leaning, paint-chipped conch houses filled with water. First it pattered, then drummed on the roofs. She had heard the most god-awful racket in the courtyard, and rose from the couch to see a comical figure, clad in an oversized orange rain poncho and carrying an oversized flight bag, sliding past her door. The figure clattered against the bicycles in the corner of the courtyard. Before he could knock, she opened the door. "Come in," she said; she could not stop laughing.

54

He tore the poncho from his back while he was still out-side, and the rain instantly drenched him to the skin.

"Why did you do that?"

"Didn't want to wet your living room," he said. He shook his head free of water, and pulled a pair of eyeglasses from his pocket. They were fogged and wouldn't do any good. His colorless eyes traveled up her bare legs, and as he noticed she was wearing only her purple string bikini, his jaw slack-ened. "I don't believe it."

"Believe what?"

"Nothing," he said.

She knew she looked good, like she had just gotten out of bed. Her red hair was piled loosely on top of her head, and she had given herself a facial that morning. Her skin glowed, too, from a thin layer of suntan oil.

After nearly a minute, he said, "Jesus, I'm sorry. I'm afraid I've got the wrong place." He tried not to look at her like she was naked, but she could see what a hard time he was having.

"I was told Benny and Annette lived here. I'm a friend of theirs from up north. Soon as it stops, I'll be . . ."

"You from Charleston?"

"No," he said. "North Florida."

"This is the right place," she said. "Benny still lives here. Annette split. She and Benny broke up a few months ago."

"Shit," Paul said. "It was Annette I knew best. I hardly knew Benny at all. I was hoping for a place to stay. I thumbed down." He showed her his thumb.

"You can stay here. Benny's at work, but I'm sure he won't mind. This place is like that. I'll ask him for you."

"If you're sure." Paul pulled off his wet shirt. His chest was milky and his ribs showed. He shivered in the breeze from the fan which was jammed in the jalousie door.

"Why don't you take a hot bath?" she said. "I'll make you a cup of tea."

"Mind if I take it in the tub with me?"

"Huh-uh."

He left the bathroom door ajar and they talked while he soaked in scalding water. She sat at the bamboo bar that divided the kitchen from the dining room. The sound of his voice did not fit his face. It was deep and harsh; his face was thin, boyish. His eyes, behind those silly horn-rimmed glasses, alternately looked old and troubled, and young and carefree. He was not really cute either, with that hairless chest as white as cold cream. But, she thought, he was hilarious.

From the tub, he told her a seventeen-year-old psychopath had picked him up on the turnpike. "At first, I wasn't sure I'd escape with my life. He began explaining some deluded vision of the world to me about meat-eaters, and not being able to kiss his girlfriend anymore because she was a meat-eater and there was a global conspiracy being perpetrated on us by the fast-food chains.

"The whole time he was talking, his left knee was jerking convulsively, and I didn't know whether to agree with him or scream for help. But it turned out that he was as harmless as your average seventeen-year-old psychopath. He was running away from home, to Mexico, to become a hermit. He had all his stereo albums in the back, no record player, and was set on finding a place with no electricity. He also told me about a planet he had visited."

"That's not so bad," Lorene had said. "I meet plenty of those."

"The worst thing," Paul said, "was what I did to the guy who gave me a ride through the Keys. A Czechoslovakian dishwasher from Miami Beach. Hardly spoke a word of English. Called it Gey Vest. He offered me pot to smoke, and I was scared as shit of him."

Lorene heard the hollow thunk of the cup dropping in the water, heard Paul curse, then heard the scattering of plastic shampoo bottles on the linoleum floor. "What are you doing in there?"

"Had an accident."

"What about the Hungarian?"

"Czech," he said. "There's a difference. He was ok, though. Until I thought he was going for my knee. I let him have a good crack across the chest with the back of my fist."

"What?"

"I thought he was going for it. You know. It turned out he was reaching for the glove compartment. I never hit anyone in my *entire* life. I almost shit. And he looked like he was going to cry. I had the hardest time explaining to him about queers and hitchhiking in America."

"I bet he didn't understand."

"I don't think he did either. And then I came running in out of the rain and was met by a beautiful lady, barely clothed."

"You must say that to all the . . ."

"I never asked your name. I mean, here I am naked in your house."

She heard him stand in the tub, the drain sucking loudly.

"My name's Fauna," she said.

"What?" He stood in the hallway with the towel knotted at his waist, and the cup in his hand. His legs were white and hairless as his chest. "Did you say Fauna?"

"I put your bag in the back room," she said as she led him down the hall. The last room was completely empty except for a single mattress set squarely in the middle of the slate floor. Tie-dyed sheets hung in the window and there was a guitar, face down, in the corner. "Early Gey Vest," she said.

"You sure Benny won't mind? I mean, I hardly know him. Are you his girl or something?"

"Not really," she said. "I just flew over from Dallas. He's having a rough time of it."

"What do you mean?"

"Trouble with his 'ex.' She dumped him, and now she's living with somebody else. Right around the street. That makes him pretty delicate."

"What do you do in Dallas?"

"Why don't you put some clothes on?" she said, leaving the room. "Before he comes home."

When he had come out of the room, he asked her again, "What do you do in Dallas?"

She had thrown an old denim work shirt on, and had let down her thick red hair so that it curled over her shoulders in the front, and halfway down her back. "I'm a dancer," she said.

"What kind of dancing do you do?"

"Exotic," she said finally, waiting for it to register on his face. There was always a change that came over men when she told them that, like declaring open season or something, and from that point on, they always acted differently toward her. She looked for it in Paul, and it didn't show. She could have told him she was a librarian, and she liked that in him.

"When's Benny coming home?"

"With him, you never can tell."

"Want to have dinner then?"

"All right."

"You pick the place," he said.

That night, they rode bicycles up Angela Street to Duval. She rode behind a while, and watched him wobble all over the place. He had nearly gotten smacked by a car, too, on the narrow streets. The mercury vapor lights and warm summer night made the evening feel unusually strange, as though they had both been transported to another world. The surreal amber light was like stage lighting. She had to lead the way, and she could feel him watching her through those silly glasses. Several times she had to wait for him to catch up while he stopped to stare into a shop window.

As they passed South Beach, a gust of pot smoke came

drifting from the burnt-out shell of a restaurant. Finally, they wound up at another place. She asked the head-waiter, dressed from head to toe in white, for a table on the dock.

Paul's eyes widened like a kid's. "I feel like I'm in a movie," he said. "You know, with Lauren Bacall or someone, back in the days when you could still go to Cuba."

Behind them, a small crowd of casually dressed locals milled around the bar, an outdoor affair covered with a bright green and white canopy. The waiters floated briskly around the tables, dressed in white tennis shorts, white shirts, shoes and socks. Their hair was sun-streaked, and all of them were limp-wristed and bitchy as hell.

They ordered cocktails and she was catching Paul's exuberance. She could smell the salt on the ocean spray now, and the tablecloths snapped in the breeze. "God, you're right," she said. "It does feel like an old movie tonight. Look at the sky." She pointed over his shoulder.

It was a rainbow of pastels, brushstrokes. The bright orange sun was slipping into the last indigo pocket of clouds, and past the horizon. She was beginning to feel human again. New. That bastard Benny had been drunk from the time she got there, and he no more appreciated her than a rock. Once, he was so drunk, she thought he was going to beat her. She would not tolerate being marked up, and she told him so. That sent him into a rage. All she had wanted was to be his for a little while, a short rest from the life she had been living. But right now she didn't care if he got carried off by a roving band of gypsies.

"Tell me about your dancing."

At first, she said no. She always told them no. But she had liked him so much now, had felt neither threatened nor part of some bizarre fantasy of his, that after her second cocktail she had said all right.

"But when I say no more," she cautioned him, "we end it."

"Fine."

She told him about where she had come from, and where, if she stayed, she was *not* going to. A friend of hers had left first. Gone to Vegas. Meanwhile Lorene—the name her mother stuck her with—began studying commercial art, but she couldn't take the teachers. They had all wanted to get her in their offices and bend her over their desks.

"By the way," she said, "what kind of work do you do?"

"Teacher." A self-conscious flush colored Paul's face.

"Anyway, there was no point in going the school route. Then Brenda came back to visit. Brenda had been good-looking enough—long legs, big chest, decent face—but when she had come back, she was gorgeous. You could see it in the way she carried herself. That night, I tried practicing it myself, and the next day, I asked her, 'How can I get that way?' "

Brenda had told her she was on her way to New Orleans to become an exotic dancer. She had had it with Vegas. In New Orleans, all she would have to do was get up on stage and peel—to music. And if the big money liked her, she could turn a trick for an extra hundred bills on the side, but only if *she* felt like it. "You write your own ticket," Brenda had told her. "That's what it's all about."

So Lorene went along. Her first performance *was* her audition. The manager, a small, balding man with heavy pouches under his eyes, had given her a kelly green sequined outfit, said her name would be Delilah, and that if the audience liked her, she could have $250 a week.

"I watched Brenda go on before me. She strutted out there on the runway, keeping almost perfect time to the music, which happened to be a record player run by the manager backstage," she told Paul. They ate Chateaubriand, new potatoes and asparagus. They drank several more cocktails, and once, as a joke, Paul went to pinch the waiter's ass and spilled his drink.

"When it was my turn, I tried to imitate the way Brenda did her number. I really got dizzy up there, looking down. I couldn't make out a thing except the lights. Clouds of smoke were whirling around in the red stage lights. As soon as I got to the end of the runway, my mind went blank. I said to myself: Lorene, honey, what in the hell are you doing?

"Once I could make out some faces, I was all right. They looked like so many pale moons bobbing in the darkness. I even tripped once, but I caught myself. And then I found a rhythm. I can't explain it. I could just feel everything inside me start to dance, not like I was part of the music, I *was* the music, and I knew I had them."

The second night, the manager suggested that she find a prop so she wouldn't feel so stupid out there. In the dressing room, before she went on, she studied her face in mock ecstasy in the mirror. She practiced: using her eyes, her thick lips, wetting them; flaring her nostrils, raising her brows. Sultry, innocent, hurt, savage and—for the end—fulfilled. She chose a long, stuffed green-and-white snake, and she imagined herself an Eve of sorts.

When she went out, she toyed with the snake between her legs, wound it around her, put the pointed tail in her mouth, humped against it, and when she was done, threw it into the audience.

The boss found her an apartment in the French Quarter and bought her a new snake every night. And every night, she felt she had done something a little different with it. And every night too, the last thing she did, after slowly and ever so provocatively removing her sequined tin pasties and matching G-string, while she lay there on the divan, working her haunches higher in simulated orgasm, the snake wiggling between her legs, the last thing she would do was kiss it, then let it fly. The place went wild.

She danced there till the club changed hands and her new boss wanted to lay her. He wanted to lay all the girls. She had told him to keep his paws to himself. She made it a policy never to sleep with bosses. He persisted and she left. Said good-bye to Brenda, who *did* lay with the boss and wound up with top billing and her snakes, even though she only walked out and posed with them, occasionally humping the curtain.

"In Charleston's where I met Benny," she said. "And the weirdest specialty act I've ever seen. I don't know if you're ready for this, you look pretty drunk."

"I can take it," Paul said. "What's a specialty act?"

"Her name was Hava Ball. No, it's too weird. I can't, and I'm not just being cute about it."

"It's not fair to say you won't tell me now. I'm fascinated. What a world!"

"I don't know how to take that." The sun had set behind Paul, leaving the sky a deep indigo with slashes of crimson like open wounds across it. The waiters whisked out whitely on the breeze and lit the overhead paper lanterns.

"Hava used to come out with hardly anything on which, if you are a stripper, is a little difficult because you don't have a lot to work with. Anyway, when she finally got down to her skin, she'd work right up to the edge of the bar, shoving herself practically right in some customer's face, grinding away. She called it 'pumping sex.'

"Benny loved it. He gave her top billing, and all the navy guys from the base and the marines came there. She wasn't that great a looker, but she had a reputation. She would begin rolling her stomach muscles like a belly dancer. She'd drop to her knees, then fold flat to her back, her head raised, and she'd spread her legs. By then the house was screaming. She'd rub herself some, and work her tits up so she could tongue her nipples. Then there was a sound like an air pistol popping and a ping-pong ball would shoot across the room. The place would go numb, so that the next time she let one loose, you could really hear the thwock, and see it fly from between her legs across the room. She had three of them inside her, and the last one went the farthest because she had the most pressure behind it, and the jokers at the bar would start balling up money and throwing it at her. She called them shooting stars."

"Bullshit," Paul said.

"Suit yourself. That's where I learned to hustle a drink. Nobody could follow that act, so the rest of us girls would do the warm-up, then get those clowns to pay as much as fifty dollars for a bottle of champagne while she was dancing. But the heat came in and busted her."

"Shooting ping-pong balls is against the law?"

"No. But one night she got too close to this ensign and nearly put his eye out. After that, Benny made her do straight strutting and she couldn't cut it. I heard she ended up with a carnie somewhere."

"Jesus, that's depressing," Paul said. "Maybe I wasn't ready for that." There had been a sparkle in his eyes, probably from the bizarreness of what she was telling him, and she saw it fade as if it were possible to be too bizarre. "What are you going to do when you can't dance anymore?"

"I don't know. I try not to think about it."

They left there and bicycled the breadth of the island. The air, once they left oceanside, was warm and muggy. They went to the Pier House and drank piña coladas. She was aware of toying with Paul, and of him not knowing the difference. He bought her drink after drink, paid for the dinner, too. The money rolled out of his pocket, and she could not stop herself from doing what came naturally—from pulling it out of him with a smile or a turn of her shoulder. She felt guilty because she knew he did not have a chance to see what she was doing. She saw it as one of her flaws, but one that she could live with.

Toward the end of the evening, she saw the question in his face. Absolutely inevitable. It always came to that, and she tried to save him the embarrassment of asking by saying, "I never dance when I'm not on stage. You know, mixing business and other things."

For the entire week, he threw his money away on her. She did not sleep with him, nor did she intimate that she would, except in the ways that she got him to do things for her. She would remind him as often as she could that she was down here to help Benny out, and Benny was important to her. She had a chance with him and she thought she better take it. That's what you do when you can't dance anymore.

Benny worked primarily at night and slept all day. She had been used to the same schedule, but since she was not dancing, she was becoming a day person again.

She and Paul went to the beach every morning and lay side by side on towels. He would put lotion on her back and down her legs. The pressure of his hands became insistent sometimes, as if it was his way of telling her how much he wanted her, but he never mentioned it in any other way. And when he finished rubbing the lotion, he would have to lie stomach down.

In the afternoons, when the South Beach regulars got off work they would play volleyball. Paul would get on the other team and watch her, as most of the other players did, when she jumped after the ball. For lunch, they rode their bikes to the Green Turtle and would sit under the wooden-blade fans in the semi-dark, eating a steaming bowl of unpeeled, boiled shrimp and drinking beer. Or they would ride to the Cuban restaurants and eat bread and black bean soup. Once, they put their money together and chartered a fishing boat. The guide took them bonefishing, and she caught a dolphin by mistake, by chance. That night, she cooked it in beer and onions under the broiler, and they sat out under the casuarina and banana trees in the courtyard eating it. It was the only time Benny had been around in the daytime that week. He groaned a lot and sat glumly in the corner. She wondered what her attraction was to that man. He talked about getting some mescaline later that week, and she said she wouldn't have any part of that garbage.

Sometimes Paul would bring books to the beach, and while she drifted into semi-sleep, the sun roasting her body, he would read her stories. He told her stories too, about the great writers. He told her about articles he was writing about them, or would write soon. She said it seemed awfully frustrating to her, writing about what other people did or meant to say. He said he didn't care what anybody thought, he liked it.

Before dusk, they would ride down Duval to the Cock 'n' Bull and sit there in the barrel chairs at the open windows, watching the people head to Mallory Pier to watch the sunset. She had never seen such a conglomeration of misfits in one place—except on 42nd and Broadway. Paul loved it too.

On a couple of nights, they followed the people to the pier. As the sun burned itself out against the line of the horizon, wild cheers went up; even Paul cheered. Then they watched the cardsharps draw people into rings around them, suckering bets out of the sun-bleached tourists. She had to explain to Paul how each of the shills worked the crowd. There were jugglers too, tanned and electric-haired, and singers, dancers and acrobats. She saw an innocence struggling inside Paul, and she found herself caring more and more for him, wanting desperately for it to rub off on her. Nobody had ever offered to take her to Audubon's House, or to Hemingway's. She got the biggest kick out of going even though she didn't give two shits about either of those jokers.

Once in the burnt-out shell of a restaurant on South Beach, the place they passed every night where the smell of marijuana smoke was as prevalent as the smell of fish, they kissed. She felt like she was in high school all over again. It was stupid and nice at the same time, like so many things about her life. They hugged tightly and her tits nearly popped out of the top of her sun dress. He palmed her shoulders, moving down to the round tops of her breasts, and she said, "Come on." It came out sounding like a reprimand and he flushed.

He asked for something foolish.

"I've been dancing for seven years now," she said. They had finished their kissing. He had a lump in his pants and he pressed up against her. "I can't quit. I don't want to quit. I make more money than I ever thought I could. I spend it like a fish. I don't have any education. Nothing to fall back on, except my body." The reasons tumbled uncontrollably off her tongue, and seemed uncomfortably like excuses now. "Someday it's gonna be gone and quite frankly I'm scared."

"Come with me then," he said.

"I can't."

"We'll get married."

That's cute, she thought. "I'm like a junkie," she said. "I could quit for a while. I know other girls who have. But they're never quite happy; they always go back. I used to hope that some straight would take me away."

"Is that what I am?" His face was a mixture of arrogance and pain.

"I'm sorry," she said. "I didn't want to hurt you. I just never really believed in Lancelots. It was something I thought about to make what I was doing easier. I have to live with being a stripper and that's the game I've invented. You have to live with being a teacher, and those articles are your trade-offs."

"Is it Benny?" Paul asked.

"Partly, I suppose. I want him, a little, but I feel dim about that too, and I don't even know why I care about him. Except he owns the clubs I work in, and that'd make me different from the other girls."

66

That night Benny did the mescaline. Paul was gone. There was a blue light on in their bedroom, and she was sleeping alone. She heard the door fly open and hit the wall. The jalousies exploded on the terrazzo floor. He flew through the house moaning deeply, a death wail. He scattered the lamps and overturned the lobster-trap end tables. He sobbed uncontrollably, calling Annette's name, and yelling, "Freaky. Motherfucking freaky." Finally, when she had him calmed enough, when she had him believing everything would be all right and there weren't things crawling his insides, when she felt helpful and useful to him, he beat her.

He threw her around the room and marked her good. She fought him back, but he had an insane strength. Though he was not a big man, he picked her completely off the floor and heaved her through the already broken door. Then he ran out of the house, disappearing in the night.

She met Paul at the airport the next day as he was about to catch his plane. She had her bags and she said, "Can I still come?" She didn't care where.

□   □

She met Donny more than a year after she and Paul started living together. On the plane, Paul asked her if she thought they ought to get married. She said, "Do I have to?" He never asked her about that again, and they had agreed to tell everyone around campus that they were.

For a while, she managed well. They took a small wooden house, a white one, in a remote section of town. It had a half-picket, half-wire fence around it and seven trees in the front yard. There was a carport and a screened porch attached in the back. She was comfortable and secure there, and she had become bored.

She had been used to a lot of money and the frenetic energy of big cities. She drew on that energy, translated it into body movements. Here, she began to feel sluggish. The salary Paul made at the university was a full half less than what she was used to, and she felt like she was pinching pennies.

Paul's colleagues all lusted after her too. Every time she visited campus, his office filled with bespectacled, musty-smelling men. She could never figure out what they were talking about, and often thought that it was all double-talk just to get a chance to look at her tits or her ass.

She took up macramé, for a week. Then guitar. She tried taking a dance class, but the women were all overweight and they eyed her suspiciously. They would cluster in twos or threes, and she would not have to see them staring to know they were watching. She had become an expert on knowing when people watched her.

When Paul wasn't at the library researching for his articles, he was out with his Group watching birds in the woods. He started expecting her to fix him dinner every night and she was about to tell him that that was too much. She was oil to his watered-down world and she wondered if she wasn't going a little crazy. This was, after all, the world a lot of women wanted.

Then Paul came home with Donny one night. She saw a glint of recognition in his eyes as they were introduced. Her whole dinner was upset by the unsettling way he continued to look at her. It was not like the fat women in the dance class, nor was it like the fossils at the university.

After dinner, Paul left the table and went to the bar to fix them a brandy. Donny leaned across to her, placed his warm hand over hers and said, "It's been a long time now, hasn't it?"

She pulled her hand away. She thought for a moment that this was just another pass, but he had a leering look in his small green eyes. "I don't know what you mean."

"Fauna, right?"

She caught her breath, looked to where Paul was, then said in a low voice, "Come on, what is this? Do I know you?"

"Dallas. The Cameo."

Christ, she thought, that's all I need.

"You oughta remember me, but I don't expect you would. I spent almost five hundred dollars that night, buying drinks and watching you do your *thing*." He emphasized *thing*.

She called up faces, men she had toyed with in the semi-dark of the clubs, getting them to spend their money like they didn't care, getting them to try to impress her, and finally getting them to take her with them. But the face that smiled at her from across the table, not an unattractive one, would not surface from the montage.

"Please don't say anything about this to Paul."

"Doesn't he know?"

"Of course. But knowing it, and knowing one of your friends knows it, is quite a different thing."

"Why don't we talk about this another time?" he said, finally removing his hand from hers.

The rest of the evening she tried to stay away from him. She pretended to busy herself in the kitchen, and she heard music inside her head. She didn't like this guy, but at the same time, the touch of his hand, the way he leaned over the table to talk softly brought back something a lot more interesting than anything she had right now.

She thought about Benny, and wondered if the letter she had gotten from her sister was true. He had opened up another club in Charleston and he had feelers out for her. He wanted her to manage his girls.

The following week, Donny invited her to lunch and she accepted. She had told him that they would have to meet near his place because Paul's students were everywhere.

He chose Harrah's Bar. Inside, it was dark and paneled with raw pecky cypress. The place smelled vaguely of wet rotting wood and flat beer. Donny talked incessantly. He said he couldn't understand how a woman with so much on the ball got hooked up with such a mope, and in *this* town. He talked about her dancing in very flattering ways. In the half-light of the bar, the lines of his face took on a nagging familiarity. She *had* seen him before. Now it was a matter of fitting the puzzle together. When they finished, he gave her a small silk cachet with an ingot of gold inside. "Have a necklace made for yourself."

They met for lunch often after that, and she had begun to like him in the way she had first liked Paul, and Benny, and the others. He made her feel good about herself, good enough to begin thinking that this thing with Paul was a respite from her dancing, and that if she didn't go back, she would lose it.

One afternoon, Donny asked her if she wanted to see the lake he lived on. It was after they had had three cocktails and she was depressed as hell. She had gone to the bookstore downtown, where they ordered the *Dallas World* especially for her. She had read that one of the girls she worked with once, even roomed with for a while, had been killed. A sickie had caught her after a show and cut her up. She had a kid, too. The whole bad dream of Sara Halfacre replayed itself inside her head; she could not shake it, nor turn it off, and by the time it had played itself out, she felt raw and scared. She wanted to be there, though there was nothing she could have done.

They sat on the dock in plastic chaise longues, drinking more whiskey and water. Though Donny complained that the heat was unbearable, its intensity was absolving to her. It melted the ice in her tumbler and seared her uncovered scalp.

Donny sat close; he took off his shirt. Since he had taken to buying her gifts, he felt free enough to touch her when he talked—a slight pressure of his hand on her knee or arm. At first he was unsure, then he grew bolder, letting his hand stay longer or pressure harder. She was used to men running their hands over her, though. It made them think they were getting their money's worth; she did not recoil as another woman might. She enjoyed it also for the memories it brought her, and she knew what was coming.

Sipping his whiskey, Donny said, "This place is so secluded, I often swim naked here."

"I don't want to go skinny-dipping," Lorene said, shutting him off. But she felt half drunk from the sun and liquor, and was in a mood to do anything that would make her feel better than she did.

"I wasn't asking. I was just making conversation." He was defensive and he looked away to the far bank of trees. "See that big, dark bird . . ."

"All right," she said.

"All right what?"

She stood up suddenly, dizzily. The light changed with her movement and she nearly lost her balance. She peeled her blouse off in one motion; her tits swung free. Her smooth shoulders moved rhythmically, and she could feel his eyes, like fingers, run over her naked breasts. Her nipples raised shyly. She was crazy drunk and altogether new again. She let her jeans fall, stepped out of her clogs, and dove in before Donny knew what was happening.

She swam for some time underwater in the undefinable cold freedom of her nakedness; the water totally caressing her, curling into her. Finally, when she thought her lungs were going to burst, she broke the surface and gave a shrill cry.

"It's great. Come on in, you lecherous bastard." God, she had to be careful. She felt good enough now to throw everything away again.

Donny couldn't get his pants off fast enough. His body was nice enough, she thought. Tanned, muscled, a little short and too wide at the top. Not much of an ass. She did not care

71

about his face then. It could have been anyone's, though it was handsome enough too.

After the swim, they lay on the dock. The warmth of the planking against her back felt splendid. The sun stretched her skin as it dried the beads of water. Each breeze that blew across the lake raised goosebumps on her belly. Donny lay stomach down, his cock hard as a board.

Later they went to bed. Afterwards, Donny said, "You're good. You know, when I was with you in Dallas, I thought: this cunt's mission in life is to give as many men as she can a hard-on."

It was a crock of shit, but it sounded good as a reprieve. He could have been a one-eyed dwarf and it wouldn't have sounded any better. She tried to remember just how desperate she had been when she decided to go with Paul. "That's very flattering," she said.

"It's the truth, Fauna."

"Paul asked me not to use that name around here."

"I don't think of you any other way. Besides, what's he got against it?"

"School."

"Doesn't that burn you up?"

"More now than it used to."

He rolled over on top of her on the daybed and started kissing her. "What made you choose it? Your eyes?" He gently kissed each one, then her neck, alternately biting and sucking.

"Partly," she said, thinking: What's a nice girl like you . . . She loved it; she loved the feeling of the strange lips running over her now. She looked past the screen and the fishing rods at the thick, shiny leaves of a magnolia tree.

"What's the other part?"

"Not now."

He stopped kissing her breasts. "Now," he said, then

dropped his head lower, to her flat tanned stomach, and tongued her navel.

"It's a nickname I used to call a girlfriend of mine. She got killed and I wanted to remember her. I think it's morbid as hell now, but I was younger then. Anyway, I got too much invested in that name to dump it and start another." It had gotten to the point once, right before she went to Key West, that whenever she saw her name on a marquee she would freak, thinking of Sara, and she would not be able to dance.

"Will you dance for me sometime? Just for me?" Donny had buried his face now between her legs.

"Maybe," she said. "But I need my costumes."

"Can't you dance without them?"

She pushed him off, got out of bed and went into the bathroom. After brushing her hair out, she got in the shower and turned the jets as hot and penetrating as she could stand them. Donny came in too.

"Did I say something?" he asked, sliding in behind her. He soaped his hands and cupped her breasts.

"No."

Then he started working the soap into a fierce lather and she said, "Stop."

"Whadda you mean stop, we just . . ."

"It'll ruin my skin."

"Soap?"

"I need lotions," she said. She liked the way that sounded—whorish. "Bath gels. Shampoos, too."

"I'll get them."

□ □

She had fallen asleep on the couch with another brandy on the end table beside her. The first rays of morning sun shone on her face, and when they began to burn, she awoke with a start. Her mouth was dry and foul from the brandy and her neck ached from twisting against the arm of the couch. She felt as if she had not slept at all, as she used to feel when her nights went queer and lasted much longer than they should have.

She looked through the house for him, mechanically checking his study first, then the bedroom. The clock on the nightstand read 8:30. She dialed his office and hung up after three rings, then called Donny.

"He won't be in all day," his secretary said, "with the campaign winding down and all."

"Where can I find him? It's important."

"I doubt you can."

"Don't give me the runaround, damnit. I'm not some dumb country hick. Where's he gonna be?" Her voice rose two octaves.

"He's giving a breakfast speech at the Holiday Inn, has a mid-morning court date, and a luncheon at the university," the secretary said. "Take your pick. If you'll just leave your name and number, I'll give him the mess . . ."

She hung up. The little fucking snip, I'd like to rip her ears off.

When she called the police, they sounded bored and told her that she would have to come in to make a formal report to Officer Roberts, the Missing Persons Department.

It felt good to shower. The warm water washed away the terribly confusing night. She stood propped against the white tile wall, staring at the designs, letting her mouth fill with water, then spitting it through her teeth in concentrated streams toward the ceiling. That prick Donny. He's convinced he's the end of the world. He's not even a good fuck . . . She scraped herself with the loofah sponge and brought the peppermint oil soap to a lather. Maybe Paul had gotten mixed up with that Brown kid. He had said something about having smoked pot with him for the first time, and that he wanted to get some so they could do it together. Who knows what he could have been talked into. The kid probably got him to take some exotic drug and they're both off in a hospital somewhere. That's the first thing she would have the cops check. Ain't life a ration, she thought. She would have liked nothing better now than to be breakfasting with Benny's pudgy dark face at the Omelet Stand in Key West, sipping white wine and reading the newspaper.

□ □

Officer Roberts' face was overlarge and ruddy. His white uniform shirt pinched the sagging skin of his neck and he constantly tugged at it. She could see the veins, small red "Y's," at all manner of angles in his nose and under his eyes so that they formed an intricate little tapestry. What a fine hunk of man.

"Can I be brutally frank with you, Mrs. McGavin?" His breath was sour, and it seemed like the only smell in the white, soundproofed room.

"Certainly."

He leaned across the metal table. "Have you and your husband been getting along lately? Problems?" It smelled as though something had crawled inside him and died. She noticed that if she followed the Y's, like a map, she could trace a route from one eye over the bridge of his nose to the other, without breaking off. She felt the room closing in on her, the walls blending together so that there were no more corners.

"You can be honest with me," he said. "Nothing will go out of this room."

"I'm telling you the truth. Why does that matter? He's missing and it's your job to find him."

"It happens frequently. Please try to be calm. The hus-

band and the missus have a spat, and he's gone for a week."
He looked at her breasts, and she could see his brain working over that line: how *he* would never be gone . . . "Then
he comes . . ."

"For Christ's sake. Do you have this spiel memorized? I
don't care what happens all those other times. Paul keeps
his appointments. He didn't show up where he was supposed
to yesterday when he left the house."

"All I can do at this point is check the hospitals for you.
But they'd have most likely called you."

"Thank you." She felt relieved after that enormous con-
cession, like some of the weight had shifted from her, even
if he did nothing for her.

"I'm not trying to get out of my job, Mrs. McGavin. You
understand that." He looked at her chest again. "It's just
that if he ain't on the top ten crime list, there's a slim
chance of finding him. Even if we could afford to saturate
the department with pictures. Some people just want to get
lost and they'll be found when they're ready. That's the way
it is."

As she was leaving the room, Officer Roberts called behind
her, "Not that that's the case with your . . ."
She thought of calling Donny again, but would only get
that snippy secretary who thought she was guarding Henry
Kissinger, and probably came at the thought of it.

As she got in her car, she knew what everything was beginning to point to. She had known it last night, and it had
really hit home with her when she was talking to Officer
Roberts' face in that cell of a room. She wished she had not
invested so much in Paul. She cursed herself for not being
able to say: fuck it and split. She had constructed these traps
now that were springing around her. They were intricate
and based on things like love, though not really love. And
fear—that was the real part, the part that made you crazy.

She decided to go home and wait, though waiting was something she found herself incapable of doing. She started making a mental list of things to do, and repeating it to herself so she wouldn't forget. "Get help" was at the top of the list.

CHAPTER

4

OWEN DECIDED TO RUN. HE HADN'T GIVEN ANOTHER ALTER-native a second thought as he lay there, swinging listlessly on the porch hammock, watching the shadows change as the moon moved slowly through the trees. It was only a matter of the correct time. He had always run before, and he could not now give himself enough reasons to stay.

He could feel things closing in on him. He felt it first in the bedroom. No sooner had he pulled the sheets over him and turned on the fan than the room began spinning, just as if he were drunk. But he was not drunk. The fan would not cool the air and his mind would not stop twitching with insane possibilities. So he moved out on the porch.

It still smelled of fresh paint. He had done it in a gloss white, and the horizontal shadows of the slats in the wood wall formed bar on top of bar. Crosby's wicker chair and magazine rack filled one corner, and in the darkness looked like a squat and sulking human form. Insignificant things had begun to take on haunting proportions to him. He worked the events over in his head. He thought smoking might help him relax and get to sleep, but he did not want to chance its opposite effect. It could make things so unbearably acute that he'd snap.

The first light of morning broke red over an eastern stand of slash pines, then faded yellow. He could hear the cocks crowing mightily in the yard now, and he could even distinguish their voices.

His back ached when he got up from the hammock. He sat in Crosby's chair, and with a mirror, changed the dressing on his eye. The skin around his brow was gathered, pink. The upper lid was nearly swollen closed, and whenever he looked at it, his balls drew up and his stomach churned sand. It replayed inside his head again and again—the absolute thunder of wings, the flashing of the yellow armored talons and the burning, blinding pain.

His neck was stiff now too. At first he thought it might somehow be related to the eye, but then he remembered Donny punching at his face and how hard he had had to move his head back and forth. It could have snapped right off his neck. The muscles were completely strained.

He should have run several times yesterday, but at some point his mind stopped working and he didn't remember when it clicked back in gear. He should have listened to his body and run when he was standing there on the porch, when he saw Paul's head jerk under like a cork on a fishing line.

And he had another chance when he was in the bedroom. Yes, he thought, there was an instant when he could've gotten out. But his body hadn't been working. It was smelling, it was seeing, it was feeling, but it was not acting. The chain had slipped the sprocket.

After dressing, he walked through the dew-wet yard to the abandoned chicken barn. Once the old owners of this farm must have kept thousands in there. The tin-roofed barn smelled foul from eons of stratified chicken manure. Now he and Crosby used it to store feed and tools, and periodically he would fill Crosby's truckbed full of the manure and spread it throughout the garden.

They kept their chickens in a small coop near the vegetable garden. Owen spread their grainy food in the bin and watched them scramble about his feet, the cocks kicking up sand around the perimeter of the hens.

He collected a container full of eggs and balanced them on the gate. Before going back to the house, he took a pitchfork and spread compost throughout the rows of the garden. He had told Crosby that he would help burn off a section of pasture, but that would have to be done another time, and by someone else.

Running seemed to be the great and controlling paradox of his life. He had run when his mother died. He had not even stayed for the funeral, and though he blamed it entirely on his father, he knew there was more to it than that. The more to it was: the sonofabitch had killed the woman with his sleazy affairs. When he showed up at her funeral with one of his sloe-eyed, slack-jawed alky woman friends, Owen had gotten right up in the middle of everything and walked out.

He left college twice. Ran. For no other reason than simple frustration with what he thought was the inanity of it. And when he cut the ties that constricted him, the pendulum upended and the full weight of the other side of the paradox dumped on him with devastating force. What about finishing things, it said to him—what about seeing one thing through before you run? These times were the real links in the chain of his life; the times when he would grab anything, the next thing, like a drowning swimmer, and hope that it would carry him somewhere better.

When he left college the second time, he grabbed the Movement. Christ, he thought he was lucky to still be alive, free of jail, or of so many of the consequences that that bullshit had brought. He had just started coming into his own, feeling like a human being, intensely drawn up in his own new ability to act. To do nothing else. He could trash a street, rip off a store. He even stole dynamite and ran guns to the Weather underground, and he had no feeling about any of it. He just did it and drew his energy for life from the immediacy of it.

There came a point, though, the inexplicable point in time when the frenzy and the sheer pointlessness of it came to him, and it devastated his life.

During the May Day demonstrations, he had been at DuPont Circle in Washington. After a harried night in the dorms at Georgetown, after as much shouting as in a football locker room before a big game, and after much drugs too, he stood on the corner in Georgetown, trembling—not from fright so much as anticipation. Everyone was going to get arrested; they would shut down the government; they would finally do something. Everybody except him. He would not let himself be drawn by the rhetoric into any grand scheme. He was merely going to have fun.

The cops buzzed in on their Vespas like a swarm of bees to clear the intersection. They heaved tear gas and charged at them in full battle dress—blue jumpsuits, white helmets with face shields, white-oak billy clubs. They screamed too. It was a sound you never expected to hear from cops, the high shrill scream of madmen.

Owen ran. He heard the sickening hollow sound of heads popping under the quick swing of clubs, saw girls and boys —some of them much younger than he—crumple under the weight of their bodies, the weight of their clothes, the weight of the billy sticks.

A small girl with long hair ran beside him. She had frightened, washed-out green eyes, and her mouth hung ragged as she pumped to keep up with him. He loved her and wanted to pull her along with him and into some alley. Then he heard the thwock of wood on bone, and as he turned to look over his shoulder, he saw her going down.

Panic numbed his mind. He wanted to run faster, knew he should have stopped to help her—that's what he had always been taught—but knew something much deeper too. He was scared for his very life.

When it was over, the streets somewhat calmer than they had been, his mind somewhat calmer too, a subtle rage festered inside him.

With the sharp end of the stick he carried, he dug a brick out of the Georgetown sidewalk. He never saw the cop's face as he stood idly on the corner, tapping his billy stick in his hand, never knew if it was the same cop who clubbed the girl, never cared. From behind, he threw the brick. Hard as his arm could throw. As soon as it left his hand, he wished that he could call it back. It headed straight for that white helmet, straight and hard and fast. His blood froze in his veins and his mind seized up in a way that it had never done before. He was overcome with all the frailty and cowardice that lived in him, fed in him, made him unable to face his father, or anything else for that matter, unable to complete the simplest of things—just run, cut it all off—and he screamed a warning before the brick hit.

He wondered what the cop had been thinking about as he stood there in *that* space and *that* time. His wife, his kids, his mistress, the Redskins, the people he'd busted. All Owen heard was a bone-crushing smack. He saw the life spill out of that man's muscles as he crumpled.

Owen's brain screamed in on itself, consuming life and

time and movement. "Do something," it yelled. His eyes searched the street frantically for a witness. An excuse to run. Someone else could help. No one. He took several steps toward the cop, whose knees twitched wildly from the concussion. There was a rivulet of blood draining from the helmet—but in the end, everything said: cut the strings, cut out. He ran.

Afterwards, he could only find comfort in doing little things, pointless things he could complete. He took a false sense of pleasure in these cycles. He would work construction till he had enough money to move to another town. Then he'd take another job, work it, and move on. After all, he thought, these were cycles, no matter how insignificant, and he was completing them. They were like building links into the chain: each new one made him feel better about the ones behind. And they had gotten him as far as Crosby's.

But now he was planning to run again. He kept telling himself that he had no attachments to Paul. Nor to anyone else. Paul had merely been kind to him. You didn't repay kindness with your life. The old man had been kind, too, taken him in—though by keeping the farm running, he had paid his own way. It was not his responsibility to nursemaid senior citizens into their graves. Fuck them all, he thought. Save yourself.

He went into the pantry the old man had built onto the kitchen. It smelled of bread and crackers and No Bugs M'Lady shelf paper. He filled his knapsack with canned foods—tuna, beans, soup, corn—took several bottles of club soda, a box of rice, some of the garden's vegetables that the old man had canned himself, and some dehydrated stores that he had accumulated for his camping trips. From the closet in his room, he took his sleeping bag, and rolled a pair of jeans, a shirt, socks and a sweater into it. He gathered his toilet articles in the bathroom, taking absolute care not to wake Crosby who slept in the room nearby. Finally he took two boxes of shells for his .30-.30 from the shed on the porch and his tent, a small orange mountain tent he had stolen during his rioting days.

Outside, the morning heat was beginning to intensify. It permeated the trees and shrubs, the grass, drying the dew from everything. It brought sweat to his back immediately.

He tossed the knapsack in the back of the van, and when he got in himself, he thanked God that the inside no longer smelled of rubber.

He backed the van around the side of the house, to where Crosby kept his bass-fishing boat, and hooked it up. He didn't give two shits if he ever got his boat back from Donny. For all he knew, it was still tied to the dock where Donny left it.

□   □

Owen drove south on Highway 315, a two-lane access road that cut through to Ocala, where he turned, and after a while, passed through Eureka—a few stores, a gas pump, a Seven-Eleven. He crossed the long, monstrous bridge that spanned the Ocklawaha River.

The Cross Florida Barge Canal would have cut Central Florida in half there. Donny had called it a big political boondoggle. From the top of the bridge he could see the Eureka Dam, its concrete jutting imperviously out of the limestone bed. Barren. The Corps of Engineers nightmare. Grass-banked levees sloped high to the sides of the channel that cut a clean swath, true as a plumb line, through to the Rodman Pool.

Underneath him, the tannic-stained river wound itself darkly out of the Ocala National Forest. The thick creosote-coated pilings, banded together like the skeletons of teepees, made the hastily cleared banks seem like the encampment of giant Indians.

He tried to imagine what the lush forest would have looked like had the Corps flooded the area. The river would have lost its definition. It would be a pool now, and underneath, the vegetation and wildlife would be so much slush at the bottom. He wondered how much of the wildlife would have escaped the day they turned those flood gates open, and how much would have drowned in that first rush of water.

Drowning. He saw Paul at the end of the rope, struggling wildly. Or had he struggled at all? When Donny popped his mouth open, his breath smelled rank with death and alcohol. Maybe he just accepted it. But nobody accepted the force and power of that engine without offering some resistance. Life called for that.

He too had almost drowned once, swimming at Fire Island. A breaker crushed over the top of him as he body-surfed, and pushed him straight to the bottom. The undertow pulled him—as though two powerful hands had wrapped around his ankles—scraping face down along the sand in a rush of deafening sound and darkness. He had managed to get his feet underneath his hips and to straighten his legs. He shot out of the water like a missile. His heart raced so fast he couldn't see, and he hung above the water for an eternity, sucking air into his lungs. He sat on the beach afterwards with an ungodly fear of drowning rattling around in his chest, and couldn't bring himself to go back in; he walked around in a vague melancholy for several days.

As Owen pulled into the landing on the side of the bridge, across from Eureka, he had no trouble lining up the boat with the ramp. He backed it down. Fuck you, bastard, he thought, remembering the way Donny had given him directions: do it till you get it right. He mocked Donny's tone, and though it had been harmless enough then, it was maddening now. He could see all right with one eye, as well as that self-righteous cocksucker could see with three.

The morning had turned unbearably hot and humid. Owen's shirt plastered to his back and the inside of the van smelled of exhaust. Gnats had already begun swarming the dried fish heads on the concrete landing. Several Negroes, wearing straw hats and with brightly colored bandanas cinched at their necks, leaned toward the river at the same angle as their cane poles. Occasionally one drew out a small bass or catfish, cut off its head, and threw it aside.

Owen took the rifle and the knapsack and tucked them under the seat of Crosby's boat. Then he pulled the van into the shade of a black oak and left the windows open so it wouldn't get too hot. He had ended the Group's first trip at this landing. There had been great confusion when he tried to explain to Donny and Paul about leaving a car at each end. He had been up half the night thinking about the Group, and the things they had done together suddenly took on inscrutable meanings. How could this group of people, so innocently and harmlessly formed, end up in this entanglement of horror? All they had meant to do was gather and drink and trade eagle stories, some of the time bullshitting irreverently. Cookouts. A canoe trip. Sightings and identifications. Imbroglios with the Game and Fish Commission. Death. What the fuck was all this compared to death? What did it matter that the shells of eagles' eggs were getting thinner because DDT had been introduced into their food chains? All their intentions were meaningless. He could see that now. What the fuck would an eagle care if the Group talked about it or not? It was all a bullshit excuse to worship something, anything, to hold each of them, yes, that was it, to hold each of them together in a way nothing else could. In a way that they could remain whole within themselves and part of all the others too, and part of all nature. But that shit backfired; it was always meant to backfire. He felt now that they each had a bit of the black widow in them, sucking just so much out of each other. Paul had been the first to empty.

He started the engine and headed upriver. At first it was wide, the banks sparse. The only sounds on the river were the muted rumble of his own motor and the Negroes singing on the concrete landing. They must have stopped when he pulled up, but he could hear them now, several of them, singing strong and deep about Jesus. Owen knew now why he joined the Group. To plug one hole and hope that others would not spring up elsewhere. But they had; they always did. Paul and Donny, even the old man, they all wanted in some way to become what they were watching, to somehow transgress all natural laws and take on the characteristics that they so revered in their drunkenness or their stupid ingenuity. To become the indomitable.

The number of fishermen thinned as the river became more sinuous, until finally there were none. Owen pulled the knapsack from under the seat, took out a joint and lit it. He cut the engine and began drifting in the direction from which he had just come. The bow righted itself with the current and snagged on a peninsula of hyacinths. He could feel the knotted jumble of his belly begin to loosen as the smoke worked on him. Somehow it had always relaxed him, helped him forget what he wanted to forget, but now even smoking became something else. Something true. It was yet another way he had devised for himself to run.

The morning was still and he listened to the silent hum of the river. Jays bickered with mockingbirds in a branch above him, each voice arrogant, self-important, screeching. The pastel purple flowers that raised out of the blooming hyacinths contrasted sharply with the stark brown water. Twigs crackled in the underbrush—deer or possum. He finished half the joint and tried desperately to clear his head of Sunday. He thought the river would give him solace. His world was unraveling before him in a series of poignant relationships—revealing itself like a deep gash. Not fatal, just open enough so he could see the pink tenderness and a little of the bone underneath. He felt poised on some inexplicable brink; the chasm below was dark.

Along this river, he had organized the trip for the Group in which Paul had seen his first eagle. They hadn't put in their canoes five minutes when they saw it. Crosby treated it like nothing; he had seen a million. He pointed out edible tree barks and flowers as they paddled with the current. Elder. Water hemlock. But Owen could not get his mind off the eagle circling above them. He had almost said something to them. Asked them why the hell they had not been more interested in the bird—after all that was the purpose of the Group. He could feel the intense focus of the bird on them, could see Paul stealing glances up to it, and he was amused with the irony of it. A group of eagle watchers being watched by an eagle.

So he watched the bird himself for the longest time. He could feel his heart drawn up by the silhouette, somehow released *by* and *into* the slow deliberate circle it cut in the blue-white sky above them. It drew him out of his body. He saw the two canoes—himself in one of them—become two moving silver slits against the slow line of the river. They looked like a pair of unblinking eyes. He could hardly contain his exhilaration, and it had been Donny who said, "Paddle, goddamnit, Owen. The back man has to paddle too." It had broken his soaring just as surely as if he had been shot.

Owen cruised to Moss Bluff and came aground in the shallows. He jumped out, pushed the boat off the sandbar, and headed back downriver under the power of the current and the trolling water.

He decided to set up the camp where he and Crosby had picked orchids. He passed it once, but he wanted to make certain there was not another place along the river. He had no idea how sticky things were going to get, but if the shit really hit, and soon, he would have to be prepared. He could not go to jail; he knew that about himself better than anything else. With his freedom taken away, he would have nowhere to run. He would end up smashing his face against the bars till his brains turned to farina.

Around a bend in the river, Owen came upon a fisherman, his bass boat tied to an overhang. He smoked a pipe as he sat in his captain's chair. When Owen passed, the man lifted an endless string of bass from the dark water, and a smile broke his face.

"Great luck today," the man whispered, holding the pipe clenched in his teeth. His face was pale and crusty under a tattered straw hat. His shirt hung loosely from his slight frame.

Owen reversed the engine and pulled alongside him. The man reached inside a red and white plastic cooler at his feet, pulled out a can of Pabst and threw it to Owen.

"Mornin'," he said. "Been here since dark."

"I just came this way. I didn't see you."

"Side creek. Bonanza," said the man. He had a cretin's head. The line of his mouth was a true slit, wide and pink as if it had been drawn there. His eyes looked like two chips of coal jammed in the putty of his overlarge face. "Bonanza."

"What?" Owen said. The man's soft voice and the bubbling of his pipe canceled each other out.

"Why you think's called Yoo-reka?" The man lifted the string of bass again. A black-wet cluster with dozens of perfectly round, lifeless eyes. "On the side creek, I was."

Owen pulled on the beer. "Sure were lucky." His mind was in low gear. The joint had put him out of synch with the fisherman—with the world too, for that matter. He was starting to feel giddy; his head and neck were stiff, but detached in some foggy unreal way.

"Luck's the biggest part of it," the man said. "That and knowin' where to cast your line."

The air around the boat stank of beer, and hung in soured clouds. Smelled like a bar, the last thing he needed to smell right now.

"Could you spare me some line?" Owen asked. "I'll pay you. Some hooks and a cork or two." He stood up in the boat and jammed his hand into the pocket of his jeans. "I got a camp downriver and it never occurred to me to bring some fishing equipment."

"What happened your eye?" The man took his hat off. He opened the tackle box, and after a moment, he held out a spool, a plastic matchbox of hooks and three corks. "Fi' dollars."

He gave the man the money.

"Your eye," the man repeated, still holding the fishing line.

"Car wreck," Owen said after a moment. He couldn't bring himself to explain the truth to this fucking rummy. It was bad enough everybody he knew thought he was an asshole without asking for outside opinions.

"Too bad. Your fault?" The man released the equipment.

"Yeah. Ain't it always."

"Had a cousin once . . ."

"Thanks for the beer." Owen pushed away from the side of his boat and started the engine. He opened the throttle full, cutting a white arc in the river, leaving the man red-faced and bobbing in the wake.

His accident had been his fault, he thought, inasmuch as anything you do in your life is your fault. Ultimately. Crosby had fired him up with his talk about how inhumane it was to keep an African tawny eagle tethered at the university's teaching zoo. It was the action he had been needing all along without knowing it. The something he *could* complete.

□   □

That first day Owen had just gone there to see what Crosby was so fired up about.

He walked through the winding pine-shaded trails of the natural habitat zoo, stopping to look at the ocelots hanging limply in their trees like stuffed and spotted carnival trophies. Rabbits, pelicans and turtles roamed freely in the path.

One section housed the wolves. The keepers had constructed grassy knolls for them to roam; they tied whole sides of beef to the trees and announced their feeding time to the public. He stopped at the monkey cage where one masturbated and another bit savagely at his hand while still others huddled toward the ceiling on branches. A duck with a cancerous growth on his beak followed him, jabbering madly and pecking at the cuffs of his pants. He kicked it away.

A peregrine falcon, bluish-gray and not much bigger than a pigeon, was tethered to a stump on the trail. Its small, black-marked head was tucked deeply in its chest and it lay in the cool sand cleaning itself. A woman with a small child walked by; the falcon convulsed and shrieked. Owen saw the tiny tooth in the tip of its hard curved beak. It used that to break the neck of its prey in mid-air. It lunged but was caught back by the shortness of the tether. The woman cried, "Damn," and scurried away with the child.

He thought the bird was sick. It turned on itself and tore at its primary feathers. He decided to tell Crosby the fucking falcon was rabid, that he had seen it himself, and that they were going to put it to sleep. That would give the old buzzard something to steam about for a while.

He passed several hawks perched on leather-wrapped cast-iron rings. He was stunned at their indifference to captivity. Their yellow beaks were fading, the protruding brows softening; their eyes had grown languid.

Finally he came to the eagle's perch at a cul-de-sac in the trail He heard a shuffling of feathers before he saw anything.

The eagle paced in a tangle of underbrush and sand. From its large size he knew immediately it was a female. Her downy brown color was a perfect camouflage.

When Owen approached the railing to get a better look, she lifted on her long wings and settled on the perch with her back to him. The span had been enormous, a full six feet across. The sunlight filtered through the thick overhead branches, playing softly along her back, dappling the brown with yellow-gold jewels. There was something in the demeanor of the bird that made all Crosby's frothings understandable. She shifted on one leg and drew the other underneath, standing perfectly balanced.

He came back every day for a week. He had never gotten this close to an eagle before and it aroused an intense warmth inside his chest. He watched her armor-plated talons work the perch, curling in and tightening, then relaxing and squeezing again in some frustrated isometric. Her head and neck muscles corded as she dipped and bobbed and preened her thick chest and wings. He wanted to get close enough to take a feather she had discarded to hang on the sun visor of his van.

When Owen stared into her round yellow eyes, he saw an inexplicable accusation. At the same time, he knew it was not blame or anything else, just his own reflection. Yet the blame surfaced in him anyway as guilt, guilt for the satisfaction he had been taking at the expense of this eagle's freedom. She seemed jittery all of a sudden, and though Owen knew she had been jittery before he ever saw her, this guilt worked against him. Somehow he had gotten a burr caught in his drawers. She wanted to fly, had the power to fly: lacked only the freedom.

By the end of the week, he had convinced himself that the eagle was going mad. Sometimes, when she was balanced on her perch, a blank serenity dissolved her eyes. Then, an instant later, she would hop down from the perch and dance frenziedly around in the sand, screeching and pecking at herself. Finally, she would go limp, spent with a kind of frustration that only she knew. And it occurred to him that it would be both his duty and his salvation to let this bird go.

He came back around dusk, waiting some distance away, and watched the keepers lock the gate. He vaulted the fence with an incredible ease, an ease born from the fear in his belly and extending even to his lungs so that if he needed to, he might even be able to fly.

Inside, the entire habitat was cast in the hazy yellow light of evening. Precise gold pendants of sunshine sparkled like ornaments on the branches. Great columns of light crossed and recrossed themselves. At each cage he passed, the animals became upset. The entire zoo came alive with alarm, the animal alarm that scatters whole herds on the plains of Africa, and he felt it contained there in all the cages. They sensed his presence as something out of order, an undefined danger. He practically rode the buzzing energy to the eagle.

She watched as Owen settled on his haunches just outside the radius of the tether. He never doubted she knew he was coming. He took out his buck-knife and opened it, then edged forward till he was at the distance of the tether.

When she didn't show alarm, he moved inside the radius. He tried to think unthreatening thoughts as she watched him. His belly tensed as his diaphragm pumped like a bellows.

He thought of the speed and ferocity of the bird; he had no doubt about the stories of these eagles being able to rip an impala in two with those talons. He tried to think of nothing too. It was best to think of nothing now, but he caught himself thinking about thinking about nothing, and thought he saw in her fierce eyes the recognition of a mistake.

He inched closer.

Though he pushed everything to the back of his mind, he could not help admiring the way her shoulders changed colors in the mixing evening light. Her eyes seemed to change too, from yellow to red, like a cat's eyes in the dark, then back again to yellow. Two discs squinting in the deeply shadowed sharpness of her features.

She turned her back and was looking up in a tree above her head as Owen inched closer still. She was preoccupied with a mockingbird's taunting, its arrogant little song rattling through the branches.

Owen slid closer again, two feet from the gnarled coil of tether. As he began to reach for it, the eagle looked over her shoulder. He froze when he realized how vulnerable he was, his left arm crossing in front completely exposing his ribs and side. Her eyes held him for an instant. He had been sure that if he would have moved, the eagle would have interpreted it as an attack.

He tried to calm his breathing. It was high in his chest, and so loud he was certain that every animal in the zoo heard it. *That* had been the reason for the alarm throughout the zoo. He had been breathing like this all along, and his abdomen felt like he had rocks in it. He was afraid she would move on him before he could back away.

The eagle watched the tree overhead again. He wanted to roll backwards out of her territory in one quick move. The light sifted again through the trees, turning each tawny feather gold, then white.

He took the tether in his hand and reached with the knife to slice it. She jerked her head around at him as though he had grabbed a part of her. Slowly, he folded the leather and placed the blade of the knife inside the fold.

He did not see anything, and all he heard was the sound of wings drumming the air louder than all the alarm that had coursed through the woods. She rose in a straight shadowed motion, the line of her wings completely engulfing him, shutting out all light. A shriek enveloped him so that he did not know if it was he or the bird screaming, and it seemed as though the talons speared his face before they even left the perch. He tumbled backwards. The knife fell from his hands as he covered his face. He kicked the ground with the heels of his boots till he found himself outside the radius of the tether, and the eagle was back on her perch.

The zoo became quiet, as if everything had been taken care of. A still night now in the woods. He lay there blinded in one eye, his head writhing with a will of its own. He was conscious only of that first terrifying scream, and aware of the absolute, abject stupidity of what he had tried to do. His shoulder was warm too, wet and sticky from blood. His chest tingled and his legs were becoming chilled at the knees when he passed out.

□ □

Sometimes the measure of what a body does is the sum total of all his stupidities, Owen thought as he landed Crosby's boat. Lord knew, he could say that about himself and it wasn't getting any better. There should be an age where things get easy. Though the bank was dense with new spring growth, it was as familiar to him as a driveway. He hopped out and pulled the bow free of the water, then tied a rope from a cleat to a tree and let the boat slide back and drift in the current till the rope tightened.

He picked out his rifle and threw the knapsack over his shoulder. This was his eyrie, where he came when he needed to get away, to preen away all the bullshit that did damage to his own delicate flight feathers. He had come here several times in the last year. Often with only a sleeping bag, he'd lie in the crisp night air, listening to the sound of the woods till sleep overcame him.

He followed an almost indistinguishable path over a rise

in the bank and down into the muddy flood plain. Cypress trees and bald cypress knees the size and shape of crooked elbows poked out of the slushy bottom. Mud accumulated on the bottom of his boots and weighted them like lead. The path rose steadily until he was on high ground. The musty smell of the rotting mosses changed inside his nose to a lush, dry freshness.

At a clearing he and Crosby had used several times before, he stopped and unloaded the knapsack. A virtually inaccessible hideout. Crosby had even told him stories about people who had gone into this part of the forest and never come out. Disappeared. Paul's wife must be thinking that he has disappeared. Vanished, as surely as if he had planned it. Beautiful woman. Hard lines around her eyes. She must have gone to the police by now. Or maybe to one of the others—Donny. He had handled Crosby so coolly, he would do the same with her. Turn her over in his hand, cooing and sighing and rolling his eyes. I'm not a bad man. Your ass. Everybody is. Half a chance and the world'll show its ass. Not a bad man. Bad as cancer.

He whittled a shovel from a branch torn from a cabbage palm, then cleared the underbrush to set up his tent. He laid the tent out and pegged the corners, raised the ends and secured them to more pegs, pulled out the sides and fastened them too. He dug a trench system around the tent for funneling rain water, taking dull pride in the meaninglessness of his effort. A good rain would wash it all down into the flood plain, but he had to give himself something to do. He dug a pit for a fire and collected several large smooth stones to surround it.

He tied his knapsack, with all the food in it, up the limb of a giant live oak to keep the varmints out and wrapped a rain tarp around it to keep it dry.

One huge oak sat on the edge of the clearing; its gray branches, thick as elephants' trunks, formed an almost solid network above him. He opened a can of tuna and ate it with his fingers. The fishy smell and the taste of oil coating his tongue made him sick to his stomach. The tarp-covered pack reminded him of Paul in the back of the van. Where could you go to escape this kind of shit? When you run, you have to go somewhere, but where do you go to get outside your own skin, to escape what you see, the tricks your mind concocts for you? As if reality were not enough . . .

□   □

Around noon, Owen went to Paul's office. Paul had given him a key once and permission to sleep in there whenever he didn't feel like making the long drive back out to Crosby's.

Three of the walls were white as notepaper, the fourth was jammed with books—all shapes, all sizes and subjects and languages. A bust of Tennyson rested on a pedestal with a black cowboy hat cocked down over his left eye. Dust was packed in the lines of his face, making him look more drawn and melancholy than he was supposed to be.

From Paul's desk, under sheaves of old essays and manila folders jammed with notes, he took an ounce of pot. He did not want it found by one of Paul's colleagues and gossiped about in the lounge.

He and Paul had sat in there after the first time he turned Paul on. They had driven around the block several times, smoking in his van, and Paul had coughed wildly and complained of dizziness. Then they went back to his office where he fell into his chair and started laughing uncontrollably.

"I say, Mr. Tennyson," Paul had wheezed at the bust. His pale face was flushed red. "I say . . ."

"What *do* you say?"

"I say I have to teach a class in fifteen minutes. What in the Lord's name have you done to me?"

Paul kept removing his glasses and replacing them on his face.

"I say," Owen said, "you'll do smashingly in there."

"I say, again, what class was it that I was supposed to teach?"

"The bust, I say, the bust."

"Beg pardon?"

"Mr. Tennyson's class."

"Oh."

In the classroom, Paul had been magnificent. Owen sat at the back watching him sway with the rhythm of his own speech, lyrical as the poem he was reading.

> Tonight the winds begin to rise
> And roar from yonder dropping day:
> The last red leaf is whirled away,
> The rooks are blown about the skies:
>
> The forest cracked, the waters curled,
> The cattle huddled on the lea;
> And wildly dashed on tower and tree
> The sunbeam strikes along the world.

He read them others too, explaining how confusion and conflict eventually emerged as principles of order, and how confusion and conflict spawned of themselves chaos, unbridled fate, chance and the real meat of life. He had said that: "The real meat of life," and the stupidity of it snapped them both back into the harsh fluorescence of the cinderblock classroom. Their eyes had locked and he had seen in Paul's a glinting. The class laughed then and he dismissed them with the excuse that his throat had given out.

Back in the office, Owen said, "I think Tennyson was wrong about the eagle in that other poem."

"Tennyson? How could he be wrong about a poem?"

"You know what I mean."

"No, really," Paul said. "I don't." His eyes softened. "I'm not trying to make a fool of you."

"Well, I imagine the eagle he was talking about, in that part of the world, was a golden eagle. Hunting from the cliffs and all."

"Yes?"

"Well, golden eagles aren't fishers."

"I'll be a sonofabitch. Score one. If that's the truth, there may be an article in that. Let's ask Crosby," he said, but they never investigated it any further.

□   □

The phone was jangling loudly and when Owen answered it he found himself completely surprised. "No," he said, "I have no idea what you should do with Professor McGavin's papers. Put them in his mailbox in Anderson Hall."

He put the baggie full of pot in his pocket as he got up to leave the office. Chaos, unbridled fate and chance—the real meat of life. The phone rang again. He did not want to pick it up, but he could no more stop his hand than he could stop his breath.

"Paul?" said the woman's voice, and he slammed the phone into the cradle. Paul's name hung at the end of that question for a full second, resonating inside his head.

Another minute and the phone began ringing again. Finally, he picked it up.

□   □

When Owen got home around two that afternoon, Crosby was sitting on the wicker chair on the porch. He held a thick glass wrapped with a paper towel and rubber band in one hand and the newspaper in the other.

From the yard, he could see the old man watching him, pretending to read the paper with his head cocked at an awkward angle. The screen door squeaked as he opened it, and before he could get inside, into safe territory—his room —Crosby said, "Come here, Owen. I want some words with you."

"Not right now," Owen said tentatively.

"Right now."

He was about to tell him to get the fuck off his back. The old man's eyes caught his and locked and he could find nothing hard to push against. He said, "All right."

"Since yesterday, you've been the strangest person I've ever seen. You've been snappy and on edge and you slept out on the porch when it was cold enough to freeze the cods off a polar bear. What's eatin' you, boy?"

Owen sat on the floor beside him. He could not bring himself to push it out of his mind as he had hoped. His trip to the river hadn't given him the solace he thought it would. Going out there had always helped before. And smoking all morning hadn't put the whole affair in moral perspective either. It had exaggerated it. He knew Donny had killed, and that he had seen it and done nothing about it. So what? But somewhere beneath the packed numbness of his brain, thought and rationality consumed each other and he no longer cared about moral imperatives.

"Something happened yesterday. Out at Donny's. Before you got there. I don't pretend to understand any of it, but I was involved. And I think I made the wrong decision."

"Between you and Donny?"

"No. It's not the sort of thing you'd guess right off the top of your head."

Crosby straightened in the chair. "You have to be clearer than that."

Owen felt trapped. This called for anything but straight

answers and that's what Crosby wanted. Truly serious things were never meant to be concisely explained. It had always been his experience that clouding them in mystery not only made them easier to tell, but also gave him a shield behind which he could retreat.

"I'll be goddamned if I can understand you," Crosby continued, sucking his tea loudly through the straw. He had a golf cap pushed back off the crown of his head. He smelled as musty as his room. Like an old man, Owen thought. That flat mothball smell. The dry skin stretched shiny around his gnarled hands. Uncountable red and purple veins marked his face. He looked frail with his back rounded into the pliant wicker.

"What happened was Paul was killed," Owen said. He did not ever think he could say that to anyone, and having said it to the old man, realized that he had said it to the wrong person.

The skin on Crosby's jowls rippled. His mouth slackened. "Who? You involved?"

"No. Donny. But I saw it, and then I became involved."

Crosby's hands were trembling. "Willingly?" His shoulders and neck twitched.

"What do you mean, willingly?"

"I don't know."

"Either way it doesn't make any difference now. It can't be reversed." His words registered on Crosby's face like blows. He never would have imagined the old fuck would act like this. Then it occurred to him that Crosby contained the uncontrollable fear of his own death so entirely that it upset all his bodily functions. He might have even wet his pants.

"No," Crosby said. "It *does* make a difference. It has to." His eyes drained of color. "Paul was killed on my goddamned land." His voice snapped loose and gargled in his throat. He looked back and forth, then over his shoulder.

"You feel ok?" asked Owen.

"No, I don't feel ok. My breath."

"Relax." Owen got up and loosened his collar. He undid his belt and opened his trousers. He had no idea what he was doing; it just seemed right.

After a few minutes, Crosby had settled down and Owen told him everything. Then Crosby got up slowly and walked from the porch. Owen sat on the floor facing the empty chair. The striped cushion still held the wrinkles of Crosby's weight. Owen felt the warm seat; and as if the old man still sat there, he let the reasons and excuses tumble from his mouth and carry him away from this place and this time.

He could still hear Lorene's voice echoing in his ears. "No one will help me," she had said over the phone. "I don't know what to do." He had felt the walls of Paul's office close in on him, bright and sharp and cold.

He had been mute for a full minute. Then he said, "I'm sorry."

"There's some sort of conspiracy going on. Or maybe I'm just paranoid. I know something's going on. I have a right to be paranoid."

"Coming over there won't solve anything," Owen had said. "I can't solve anything for you."

"Tell me what you know," she said.

"I have to go." He hung up and left without locking the door.

Crosby had gone into his room and lain down. Owen waited till he thought he was asleep, then checked on him. He lay motionless on top of his marble-hard mattress. The mahogany bedposts stretched nearly to the ceiling. The room had the same musty smell that he had noticed on the porch. It was strange that he had never noticed it before. At first he thought it was the books that lined a complete wall and stretched uniformly to the ceiling. But then he realized it was the mattress, the slab Crosby slept on day and night that transferred that awful smell to him.

In the living room, Owen called Paul's wife. He asked her if he could come over. There was something, after all, that he needed to tell her. He did need to tell somebody. He realized *that* as soon as he told Crosby.

She answered the door before he knocked. "Come in," she said, and ushered him through the foyer into the living room. The drapes were drawn and a metal globe lamp dimly lit one corner of the room. She was off in some other world. He could tell she knew something. Beautiful. She was wearing a pair of tight jeans that drew inward from her legs, around her ass, to her crotch. He nearly howled when he got a good look at her breasts.

Under his feet, the thick brown shag carpet made him feel as though he were gliding above the ground. There were abstracts on each wall framed in chromium and glass. Over the wall-length gray couch, there was a single painting of smeared grays and blacks, sharply angled whites, and the artist's name printed boldly: Baron. The room felt barren. Everything was so neatly appointed, like her hair—each strand in its proper place—that he thought she must have cleaned the room several times between last night and now.

"I went to the police, you know." She glided across the room and slipped into a corner of the couch. On the glass and chromium coffee table, there was a drink. The goldness of the whiskey had gone pale. A water ring circled the base of the glass.

"Could I have something to drink?" He sat on the floor. His ass sunk in the carpet. He looked at the painting above her head.

"Beer? Brandy? Something harder?"

"Beer." You look hard enough, he thought. He searched her green eyes from halfway across the room. The silence was unbearable. She got up and went into the kitchen. Her eyes were the only bright things in the whole room. He could feel Paul's presence in the house—the austere dark colors, the preciseness of things.

When she came back in, she said again, "I went to the police." Her voice was more forceful. It held out an accusation.

"I expected you would." He poured the beer into the glass and drank it halfway down, till he couldn't stand the burning in the back of his throat.

"They didn't help."

"Look, Mrs. McGavin . . ."

"Lorene."

"Look," he said. "I don't know what you expect me to tell you." He imagined the horror and tears, expected her to be as weak as her voice sounded over the phone. He could have handled somebody weaker than him. But she charged the air with electricity, and underneath that pile of fiery red hair, she was a churning dynamo.

"What did you mean over the phone then?" A sharp edge lined her voice. "Paul was there Sunday, wasn't he? I know he was there."

"I didn't say that. I didn't . . ."

"You didn't say anything yet, but you better." Her hand shook as she took a drink. "I gave your name to the police. You and Donny and Crosby, and God knows who else, are in on this together and you better come clean of all the crap. I'll go somewhere for help. I've got connections in New York and Dallas, you know, and I'll use every goddamned one of them. I'll get to the bottom of this . . ."

Her voice trailed off, and though she was not crying, Owen could feel it behind the words. It had been happening to him too, every hour on the half hour like a bus since all this shit started. Underneath all the steel wire and cables, everyone was delicate as crystal. There were just different thicknesses.

"An accident," he finally said. The words tumbled out and he felt as vulnerable as he had when he exposed his side to the eagle. He waited for her to unleash on him. There was nothing but dumb silence. It had been like swallowing a rock but it was down now. The gray abstract above the couch revealed its form to him. The picture was a ship listing sharply in a gusting ocean. He could see now the turmoil, the unrestrained chaos, of the waves breaking over the bow.

"The hospital didn't call," she said.

Then her face changed. Her aquiline nose widened; her large eyes flared as a flush of deep pink crossed her face. She threw the glass across the room. "I knew it!"

"I didn't do it," Owen said quickly. "I couldn't stop him from . . ."

"Donny?"

The listing ship had transformed itself into the snarling jaws of a wolf. The white foam of the breaking waves had become the teeth, drawn and frothing and ready to rend flesh; then, like watching an afternoon mural of thunder-heads, the colors melded themselves back into the roiling jumble they had always been.

"I didn't do it. I didn't want to have anything to do with it at all. You gotta believe that. God, you gotta. He'd a killed me in an uncontrollable fit of rage."

She ran out of the room.

He lay back on the rug, feeling its softness rise up around him, cutting off the hum of the air-conditioner. The faint whisper of music came from somewhere in the house, and from the bedroom, he heard a muffled banging as though she were throwing everything she could lift.

"Get up," she said when she came back in the room. "What did that sonofabitch think to gain from hiding this? What do *you* expect to gain?"

He felt compelled by the forcefulness of her question to answer, but he couldn't. "I don't know."

105

"I sensed this whole thing when I talked with him over the phone. I knew it." She was not looking at him. She paced back and forth behind him. He could almost hear the crackle of static the sliding of her slippers made.

"What are you going to do?"

"Go to the police again."

"You think they'll believe you?"

"I believe me. I'll *make* them believe me."

"And if they don't?"

"I don't know, goddamnit. I don't know. But I'm not going back to the assholes that run Missing Persons. I want real cops." She stopped pacing and stood over him. Her jeans shone and he looked up to where they gathered at her crotch. "I want the elections stopped."

"You can't stop elections."

"Then I want him stopped. I'm going to take you with me to the police." Her fists were bright red as though she had been beating on the walls.

"Your ass," he said. "If I go to the police, I'll be in as much trouble as him. And I don't have the resources to deal with that."

"You're already in as much trouble as him."

"Maybe, but I'm still free."

"Tell me what happened. I have to tell them details."

"No."

"I won't mention you. I want to get Donny."

"Oh, come on. They're not stupid. They'll pick me up in two seconds. I'm not going to throw my life away." He realized, suddenly, that Donny had used those exact words yesterday.

CHAPTER

ALL SUNDAY NIGHT, DONNY TRIED FORCING HIS THOUGHTS ON the campaign. He reviewed his speech for the morning and went over his notes for the trial. He could not concentrate, and finally decided that he had no other choice but to sleep.

He lay naked on the daybed, letting the magnolia-scented breeze play over him. The leaves of the tree outside the porch were green and stiff in the waning moonlight. The dock looked like a gray path, extending over a silver mirror of lake. Owen's boat was still tied to the pilings and periodically he heard the muted bumping of the bow against the wood.

It brought him back in touch with the afternoon. He thought: why me, why now, why ever? He understood how people's lives could crumble in an instant, like in the movies. He was in a corner now and it made him sick to think of the things he would do to get out. He felt his body warm till it sweated in fever. He tried holding his eyes closed but they would begin to flicker convulsively until he was left there, eyes wide, senses reeling. He wondered if Owen would have the balls to turn him in. He could have killed him too this afternoon. For an instant, he had been capable of it. He had been capable of anything then. He had gone absolutely insane. It wasn't the distant thing that you hear about in a clinical way; it happened easily. And he was more afraid that it would happen again than he was of getting caught.

He kept muttering, "Bad doesn't have anything to do with what I've done. I don't deserve this." It was as if he were talking to Owen in the van all over again. He wanted to make him understand his life, all at once, in a way that would convince him that he was not a bad man. He wanted to make him understand how hard he'd worked, and what it felt like to be a piece of shit for so long. And then the cookies started falling in place and he had something—a little money, a little bit of a name, and a future.

But all that is not the kind of thing you can make a person understand, ever. He could not pull the words from anywhere, and all that came out was, "I'm not a bad man."

And Owen had looked at him like he was a lunatic.

In some ways, Paul had known his struggle. After all, he had somehow gotten Fauna. The thought of Paul, lying lifeless out on the dock, raised an acid hatred from deep in Donny's belly as though Paul were to blame for the turn of events.

Paul was a weakling, not physically, but in a vital way. There was no substance to the energy he generated. Killing him was bizarre. He had felt nothing for doing the act, but the consequences registered like aftershocks. Finally he had felt some black remorse poking through the shell of defenses he had thrown up. It came to him as consolation as he said the words: I'm not a bad man.

Then the phone rang and he crossed the porch in the dark, stubbing his foot on his desk chair.

"Hi," she said. He instantly recognized the hint of uncertainty in her tone.

"Hi, Fauna. How are you? How's Paul?" he said. That thing inside him, base and self-preserving, clicked on and took control of his speech, as it had taken control of his actions this afternoon.

· "What do you mean how's Paul? *Where's* Paul?"

"I don't get it. When he didn't show up here . . ."

"He didn't show up? But he left around noon. He was going straight to your place."

"Did you tell him about us?" Donny asked quickly.

"No. Why? I don't understand."

"Well, I thought that might be why he didn't come. You know he's been acting strange lately. Even some of the guys in the Group mentioned it, and so I . . ."

"Stop it," she yelled.

He did not know what else to say. He could not believe he had gone as far as he had. He wanted to somehow explain it to her and make it all go away.

"I'm worried," she continued. Her voice cracked, and at the same time he noticed his chest was trembling. He sat down in the chair and turned it away from the lake. He flipped on a lamp and stared at his map of Florida. "It's not like Paul to do something like this."

His pulse was beating in his ears as he said, "Nonsense. He probably found out about us and went out on a bender."

He did not hear the rest of what she said, nor was he aware of continuing the conversation. The next thing he knew, he was listening to a dial tone.

Her voice had whined in a way he had never heard before, in a way he would never have believed she was capable of. It was a helpless, dominatable cry. He wanted to hold her in his arms.

He left the light on when he went back to bed. He lay there with his eyes closed trying to force sleep on himself. For the time they had spent together, she had been a fantasy fulfilled. She was the kind of woman that most men dreamed of, and he had taken what he wanted from her. Then she went home to her Paul. It was somewhat like skimming the best off the top without having to pay any price whatsoever. But her voice on the phone had said price, and said it in a big way. It lashed around inside him till his cock shriveled at the thought of her, till his eyes began flickering again, and till he found himself staring wide-eyed at the crossbeams of his ceiling.

With time, he slipped into that nebulous area of dreams that preclude deep sleep. He had the sensation of knowing he was there, and the incapability of pulling out. He dreamed of Paul, his body twisted and limp on the dock. He touched him, and was touching Fauna's taut pink breasts. The sameness of texture startled him but he could not wake. He kissed her and when he drew away from her face, it had been Paul's bluish cold lips he had been kissing. He screamed but no sound left his mouth. And finally, his hardness pressed against her, he entered her from behind without taking his eyes from the sweet indentation of the line of her spine. Her thick red hair fell to the side, exposing her smooth shoulders and the delicate nape of her neck. She urged him to kiss her. He reached around to take her chin in his hand, to turn it to the right angle, and he felt coarse stubble. He woke sweating, his legs knotted in sheets and covers.

Although it was still dark, he got up and shaved. It took him forever to scrape his face clean. His hair was tousled; his eyes looked drawn and bloodshot, not sharp at all. Before he showered, he gathered all Fauna's creams and lotions, her bath gels, shampoos and loofah sponges, and put them in a garbage bag.

He went through the house, found her brush with spun webs of red hair in it, found a pair of panties, impulsively sniffed them, then threw them in the bag too. He took the autographed publicity pictures she had given him from his desk drawer—the ones where she had posed in costume and out—and tore them up. All of them except one. It was the one he liked best. When she gave it to him, he had told her, "This picture says everything about you. It shows quite a lot too." He put it back in the drawer, covering it with some manila folders.

He dressed in his favorite suit, a three-piece Pierre Cardin which fit the lines of his body—the strong shoulders, hard, flat stomach, small ass—as well as if it had been tailor-made, but even it felt loose, awkward. Dirty. He could feel the stain on the back of the shirt even though it was covered by the vest, feel the pin-sized hole at the base of his crotch. Like his dreams, these things became insistent and inescapable.

He drove to his office and read his breakfast speech aloud repeatedly, raising his voice to a bellow. Around seven-thirty, his secretary came in and answered the phone that had been ringing for five minutes.

"Excuse me, Donny," she said after knocking on his door. "It's the McGavin woman."

"I'm not here, Georgia," he said. "I don't want to see her. I don't want to talk to her. Make excuses for me."

An instant later, she came back in with a cup of coffee. His back was turned away from her; he faced a large plate glass window that overlooked his patio. He spun around as she set the cup down. "You happy, Georgia?"

She took her glasses off and set them on top of her head. She caught the end of her dark hair between her thumb and forefinger and started twirling it. "I . . . I don't know what you mean."

"I mean, are you safe. Oh, I don't know what I mean."

She looked very pretty to him just then. She wore no bra and her little tits showed pointed and dark under her white jersey. He felt like bending her over the desk, hiking her skirt and reaming her.

"You're acting queer as shit," she said. "You all right?"

"Yeah. Do me a favor and try to get hold of Owen Brown. It's the same number as Arnold Crosby in the Rolodex. Ask him to come see me. Tell him it's urgent."

☐   ☐

The banquet room of the Howard Johnson's was lined with flags. Kiwanis flags, American flags, State of Florida flags. The burgundy drapes were drawn so that the early morning sunlight streamed in parallel shafts through a wall of hedges and glass. Billows of smoke swirled in those shafts, making the entire room appear cloudy. A monotonous buzz of conversation, accompanied by the clanking of silverware on porcelain, rose from the tables. Donny was ushered in through the sliding wooden curtains to his place at the speaker's table, which was placed perpendicular to the others and draped with a purple Kiwanis banner.

He picked at his breakfast—a stack of hotcakes, sausage, coffee and muffins—while the Kiwanis president nibbled at his right ear. He agreed with what he said though he could not seem to hear it. The men at the tables eyed him suspiciously between mouthfuls of food. He had trouble keeping the focus in his eyes. The whole situation was painfully incongruous—he was about to address them on the campaign issues of integrity and law and order, among other things. If you assholes only knew . . .

There was an ovation and he felt a slight tug at his elbow before he realized that he had been introduced. He rose, placed his manila folder on the portable podium and cleared his throat.

"Thank you, Mr. President." He turned and gave an ingratiating bow to the man who had introduced him, noticing that his fat face and puffy, hanging jowls resembled a bulldog.

"Members of the Kiwanis International, good morning. I've never been quite sure that having a politician speak at these breakfasts was a good idea. Not for the people eating. If he speaks before you eat, you're liable to lose your appetites. And when he speaks after, you're liable to lose your breakfast." He waited a moment and there was some uncomfortable chuckling. They didn't go for that one and he knew he was in for it.

"I'll tell you straight from the shoulder what my platform is all about, what I'd like to do, and just how I plan to do it. First, let me tell you that my opponent, Mr. Benson, has not addressed himself to a single issue that has required an unequivocal stand. I'm not sure that he even knows municipal and county consolidation is any concern to you people."

The resonance, the convincing spitfire energy that he had had in his other speeches, was missing. The men shifted in their chairs and picked at the leftovers on their plates. He was absolutely alone there; he felt their eyes as penetrating lasers. Naked. The spot on the back of his shirt. These weren't hick farmers or college kids; they were hard-core businessmen and they'd heard the ration of shit he was about to dish out from every earthworm that ran for anything.

The environmental portion of his speech met with little more than polite approval. It occurred to him while he was talking that these men probably didn't even know what a hardwood hammock was, nor did they care about the implications of draining Levy Prairie for cattle grazing.

Donny looked from face to face, trying to find a sympathetic pair of eyes, one person he could play to. They were indifferent to him; they thought he was an asshole.

One man, sitting along the wall in the front, looked like

an older version of himself as he looked in the mirror this morning. Tousled and raggedy, with drawn, distracted eyes. The man upset him, caused the burn of bile to creep up from his belly. He kept talking, but the higher the feeling got, the more complete his own distraction became. He could feel his balls drawing upward, hardening. His ears burned and he forgot the words as they came out of his mouth.

"I'm sorry," he said. "This campaign has been very rigorous, a strain on all those involved." Everyone laughed for the first time and he couldn't figure out why. He wanted to get out of there.

He remembered when he had dumped Paul's body into the mine, the tremendous feeling of deliverance, of freedom, of giddiness that ran through him. He had really believed— in his own insanity—that it *was* all over. But his body would not let him forget it now. It was betraying him, playing tricks on him. He wanted to peel away the skin, and step out as someone new.

When he left the breakfast, he felt dismal. He drove straight to the courthouse in Palatka. Outside, he met Mrs. Barkum, the woman he was to defend. She was a hulking shrew of a woman, fat and smelling of the farm in a faded denim dress that stretched across her flaring haunches. She was the mistress in a marital feud, and for the life of him, Donny could not figure out how a man would get close enough to heave a bucket of water on her, much less bed with her. She had stabbed the wife with a paring knife. "Pay me now, or I won't step one foot in that courtroom," he told her.

"My youngen just had a baby. Let me send you the money."

"My secretary explained to you that I do not work for free. I am not a wealthy man," he said. He sounded like he was poor-mouthing and he hated himself for that, but he had

let a fortune in fees slip through his hands because he
had not gotten the money up front. He knew there was no
baby.

"But . . ."

"That's the way I work."

The clerk poked his wan gray face out the swinging doors.
"Mr. Waldo, you're up next."

The woman said, "Awright." She opened the clasp of her
purse and pulled out a ball of money. Her stubby fingers
held up the green nut of money and counted off two hundred dollars.

"After you, Mrs. Barkum," he said.

The inside of the circuit court looked particularly stark
today. The institutional yellow walls were so bland, they
made his mouth taste of sawdust. The tables, podium, jury
box and judge's bench were a year-worn maple, dull and
stained. Huddled in a corner, beside the judge's bench and
the flags, were the clerks, recorders and bailiffs—all wearing
identical forest green blazers, and each one older than the
other. Some of them were friends of Crosby's. He kept
having flashes of fear wash through him, expecting at any
second for someone to announce the jig was up. He had
never felt his existence so acutely as he did now.

He made a note to call Georgia during the first recess.
He had to check on the kid and make sure he was still
holding.

He spread his manila folder on the table, arranging his
questions, opening argument and rebuttals of the prosecution's case. He had an edge, he thought, when he had been
painstaking enough to present the case so that the jury would
see it through the eyes he provided. Somewhat like threading
a needle.

Finally the clerk announced Judge Eastmund. Everyone
rose simultaneously except for one woman. The judge had
a pink-smooth woman's complexion and wore thick horn-

rimmed glasses. He called the bailiff aside and whispered something to him. The bailiff asked the woman, in a voice loud enough for the entire courtroom to hear, why she did not rise. As she stood up, she showed a baby sleeping on her lap. The judge ejected her.

What a prick, Donny thought. He always pulled this kind of shit. He was asshole-buddies with the state's attorney's staff, and loved to jump down the gullets of the defense. Donny knew he was going to have trouble with Eastmund, and as he was not as well-prepared as he thought he should be, he became nervous.

"That's not a judge," Mrs. Barkum whispered slowly, "that's a hatchet man."

Donny waved her comment aside.

The jury had been selected early last week, and they fidgeted in the hardbacked chairs. He had been lucky to get the two black women past the prosecutor, and it cost him when he conceded the hardware salesman. The young girl who was very pretty except for her thick eyebrows sat with her shoulders straight and her arms folded across her chest as if she were impatient for the circus to begin. Bring on the dancing bears. When the judge asked for any motions, Donny waited his turn, then stood and asked for a dismissal on the grounds that the prosecution offered insubstantial evidence to convict his client. Denied. He thought of Fauna. Two calls since last night. It wasn't supposed to work out that way.

"You may sit down now," the judge said.

"If the defense attorney is finished daydreaming, Your Honor," the state's attorney said, "the prosecution would like to call its first witness."

Donny flushed when he realized that he had remained standing. He couldn't afford to make these amateurish mistakes now. He told himself, Don't be stupid, and expected some kind of resolution to firm him up.

The case centered around an ongoing family feud in Put-

116

nam Hall involving two notorious women, and had cul-
minated in the stabbing. Nothing serious. But because he
had announced himself for public office, he was being
watched and reported on by the papers; and the trial took on
an exaggerated importance for him.

The state's attorney, a dwarfish white-haired man with a
purple birthmark the size of a palm on his cheek, called three
witnesses. All had been drinking at the bar at the time of the
stabbing. Each time the clerk re-entered the courtroom, he
got a little redder as he announced that Mr. So-and-so was
not out there.

Finally, the wife was called. She limped up to the witness
stand, her arm bandaged in a dirty sling. She was a raw-boned
woman whose small eyes were separated by a wide, flat nose.
Her bleached-blond hair was knotted in a bun at the back of
her head.

The state's attorney led her through his questioning.

She identified the woman at Donny's table as, "That's a
lunatic what stabbed me."

The judge looked at Donny when he didn't object and
then instructed her himself to answer only the questions
asked.

"I was at the bar," she said. "And when I seen her, I went
right up to her and said, 'You oughter not mess with Evan.' "
(She pronounced it EE-van.)

"Is that when the defendant stabbed you?" the state's attorney asked.

"She did. That Barkum woman pulled a knife straight way
out from under her dress, between her big fat legs," she said
quickly, "and sliced on me like I was a peach or something."

"Your Honor," Donny said as he stood. "Are you going
to let this go on?"

"Take it easy, Counselor. Mrs. Blanchet, I have told you
once already . . ."

"Sorry, Your Honor."

Finally Donny got a chance to examine her. He laid his groundwork patiently and methodically from the podium. He alternately rested on his elbows and paced, not looking at her till the last word in the question. He established place and time and situation.

"Isn't it true that your husband, Mrs. Blanchet, is estranged from you?"

"Don't know what it means."

"Could you speak a little louder?" Donny said. He wanted her uncomfortable; she had been too cocky. He wanted her to think about the way she was talking and not what he asked.

"Don't know what stranged means."

"I can't hear you."

"Mr. Waldo," the judge said, "the woman is quite clear in her way of speaking."

"Where is your husband living?" He paced along the jury box in front of the podium. The girl with the thick eyebrows wore heavy perfume and he could feel her intense stare aimed at the side of his head.

"Home," Mrs. Blanchet said.

"All right. Where was he living at the time of the alleged assault?"

"With her."

"Who? Would you please indicate to the jury."

She pointed her bandaged arm.

"That arm hurts you, does it?"

"Objection."

"Sustained."

"Please restrict yourself to your cross-examination, Mr. Waldo. And get back behind that podium. I'll not have you intimidating the witness."

"Sorry, Missus Blanchet," he said. "Now if you'll just answer a few more questions."

He couldn't find his place. He rifled through the papers

on the podium. A page was missing from her deposition. "Excuse me, Your Honor." He found it in one of the manila folders on the table. Jesus, I just want to get out of here, he thought. These two biddies could go suck air for their equal justice. It wouldn't do any good anyway.

"Were you drinking on the night of February 14?"

"I s'pose."

"What does that mean—'I s'pose'?"

"I drink every night," she said. The courtroom burst into laughter.

He came around in front of the podium again. "That's right, Missus Blanchet, every night. And isn't it true that on the night in question, you were not just drinking, but were, quite literally, drunk?"

"Objection."

"Wasn't it you, in your drunken stupor, Missus Blanchet"— he looked at the jury—"who actually threatened the defendant, and wasn't it true that she was merely defending herself against your . . ."

"Objection, Your Honor. The defense attorney . . ."

"Mr. Waldo," the judge's voice bellowed above the din.

". . . drunken verbal assault," Donny continued. He could hear his voice rising with the tension in the courtroom. He was shaking his finger in Mrs. Blanchet's face. She had her chin jutting out arrogantly and he wanted to knock it off.

"Mr. Waldo," the judge shouted again, pounding his gavel on the bench.

"No more questions, Your Honor," Donny said. Sweat drenched his shirt underneath his jacket. He sat at his table.

"Another outburst like that, sir, and I will find you in contempt of this court."

Donny stood and dipped his head. "Sorry, Your Honor."

His client, Mrs. Barkum, leaned on his arm. "You was fantastic." Her breath was hot against his cheek.

The jury was out a half hour. They found Mrs. Barkum

not guilty and after the judge remanded her from custody, he instructed counsel to meet in his chambers. Donny knew he was in for a lashing. He sent a note to Eastmund's chambers, via the court recorder, that he had been taken ill and had to leave immediately.

He felt like he was nearing breakdown city and he wasn't going to give that bastard Eastmund a chance to shove him in.

□   □

The first thing Donny saw as he opened the door of his office was her clogs. He recognized them instantly. Her legs were crossed and she wriggled her foot nervously in the air. He wanted to slide out, but she had jumped at the sound of the door and their eyes were now locked. "Donny?"

Georgia had tried to warn him as he came in. She said, "I told her you weren't keeping office today." She glowered at Lorene, then turned away on her swivel chair and began typing something.

"It's all right," Donny said.

He ushered her down the long hallway into his office. He cursed himself for watching the balls of her ass roll in those tight jeans. He had never done it with her in his office and he had thought about it often. It was this same self-destructiveness that had gotten him into this whole mess in the first place.

"Want a drink?" he asked.

She wore a green wraparound blouse that made her breasts look smaller than they actually were. "Scotch," she said.

Three walls of his office were paneled. He kept his bar along the fourth, in front of a brick wall with the mason's emblem in the shape of a diamond.

"With ice and soda," she said.

He mixed the drink, eyeing her suspiciously, waiting for everything to come unraveled. She sat behind his desk and turned her back to him, facing his bookcase.

He put the drink on the desk beside her and walked to the picture window that overlooked his patio. They used to have lunch out there once in a while. "What's up?"

After an interminable silence she said, "Something's happened."

His insides turned somersaults. "What do you mean?"

"I mean something's happened to Paul."

Again there was silence. He wondered if she were waiting for him to tip himself. "How do you know?"

"I don't, for sure," she said. He turned just as she was brushing back the hair from her forehead; he wanted to tell her that her perfume was driving him mad. "No one will help me and that's a pretty good indicator. I've been to the cops and they tell me he doesn't want to be found. They say he'll come home when he's ready. I called Crosby."

"What'd he say?"

"I think he's senile."

"What about the Brown kid? Did you try him?"

"Nowhere to be found. The old man said his van wasn't parked outside. And you?"

"Me what?"

"Nothing."

"Come on, Fauna. You don't think I . . ."

"I don't know what to think. You're acting funny as hell."

"The pressure," Donny said. "You know the elections are tomorrow. I can't drop everything I've worked for because you can't find Paul."

"You callous sonofabitch," she said. "He'd do it for you. He'd do it in a minute for anybody and I can't find a single person who'd do it for him."

He expected her to break down then. He could see it coming—the hands began to flutter; her chest heaved. He hadn't meant to let that side of him out. I'm not a bad man, he said to himself, hoping to right everything.

"I'm sorry," he said. "I'm so pressured today that I think the top of my head's gonna erupt. What can I do?"

She downed the glass of Scotch, stood and wrapped her arms around his waist. "I'm scared," she said. "Hold me."

She buried her head in his chest. He could feel her tits pressing into him, could smell the strong, flowery fragrance of her perfume, her slight back heaving under his arms, and he was deathly afraid that she would raise her head to kiss him and she would have Paul's face and Paul's smell.

"This has happened to me once before," she said, "and I didn't do anything about it. Now it's happening again."

"It'll work out," he said. She squeezed, and he knew she wanted to be reassured.

She pulled away and looked into his eyes. She looked puzzled and he immediately thought, What did I do?

"I'm sorry for bothering you," she said. She drew a compact from her purse and corrected her makeup. She left without saying another word.

He waited till he heard the front door close and he pressed the intercom. "Georgia, lock up the front door."

He tried calling Owen twice and got a busy signal both times. He needed to talk, to keep himself occupied.

"Georgia, would you come in here please?"

She knocked, then opened the door before he could answer. "What's up?"

"You wanna get out of here with me? Out to the lake. We'll bring a bottle of wine."

"That woman upset you?" She leaned against the wall, her face all lighted up. Her nipples poked against her tight jersey.

"Don't be a smartass," he said. "I've got too much on my mind."

122

She crossed the room in her best fashion-model walk, exaggerated and slinky, and fell into his lap. She wrapped around him like a snake and kissed him hungrily, grinding her hips against him. He had never been so happy to smell the cigarette smoke on her breath. She raked his scalp with her nails. He thought, yes, this was the only way. He needed to have his mind taken off yesterday. And tomorrow.

CHAPTER

As CROSBY LAY ON TOP OF THE CHENILLE BEDSPREAD—THE
white one with the fleur-de-lis pattern that his wife Margaret
had picked out for them on one of their drives north—he
tried to calm his breathing. She had picked out everything
in the bedroom, and since she was gone, it was the only
place left where he could still feel her presence. Though
he had never touched a single book on the shelves that
extended to the ceiling and that she had insisted on his
getting, nor oiled the mahogany bedposts and headboard,
nor even rearranged so much as a pen on the rolltop desk
except to dust, he had been unable to hold the feeling of her
around the farm.

He had felt his blood pressure rise, pumping strong behind
his eyes, as Owen told him what had happened at Donny's.
He felt, too, a sickening duplicity for being there, for drink-

ing with Donny and talking with him as though nothing were wrong. The air on the porch had, at once, become thick and clogged at his throat. His left arm began to tingle high in the shoulder, then the numbness moved down to his pinkie and ring finger. He had gotten so scared that his legs started shaking of their own and Owen's face blurred.

Now, as his body heat warmed the bed under him, the numbness faded and he was safe. He could still hear Owen's voice drifting from the porch, rhythmic as a song though he was not singing. The kid had really made a mess of things by getting mixed up in this. The confusion registered in Owen's eyes as a dumb incredulous stare; his cheeks had a constant sanguine flush to them. He recognized Owen's complete and utter helplessness as something he had seen in his own face so many years ago. So much of what Owen was now, he had been. When Paul first brought them together, he was struck with Owen's vulnerability. It had seemed to him then that somewhere along the line he and Owen contained the same molecules of origin and that they had been seeking each other unknowingly.

He wished he could have said something to him on the porch, before his body fouled. He wished too that he could do something, but the events were already set in motion. No one could take it all away with the sweep of a hand.

If he could have grabbed Owen, shaken him senseless, he would have. There was no reason for someone as young as he to have these complications. Death was something that occupied the old.

It was what he had felt since the first time—the terrible unfairness of it all, the nagging succession of ghoulish nightmares. It followed him, awake or asleep, like an albatross.

His own relationship to death added up to a series of mistakes that he had set in motion, and the inertia of that first instance carried through with him for his entire life. And now it was happening again. That was what death was like.

One incident in time that gets some kind of center thrown out of kilter and causes a godawful series of events to be set in motion. Some people could find their balance again and side-step it, while others were caught for the ride.

The door to the living room creaked open, then closed. He heard Owen padding down the hall. He closed his eyes and pretended to be asleep. He could not talk with Owen; he could not look at his face again. Sitting on the porch, Owen had become that boy next to him in the trenches. He wore that same death-mask of startled incomprehension.

Through half-closed lids, Crosby watched Owen stand over him, then turn and walk to the bookshelves. He climbed the spiral ladder and ran his hands along the books. He stood there too long, and Crosby saw through the dim flickering of his own vision the faces of them all—the boy in the trenches, Margaret, even himself. Before he could say any-thing, before he could tell Owen to get out quickly or else he too would become a face in the stockpile of his night-mares, the bedroom door clicked closed and he was left alone with the cold humming of the air-conditioner.

They had been in France for only a week. His unit had been whisked by train from the port, through the dank-smelling cold cities where clusters of gaunt-faced old French-men gathered at the stations, shaking their fists at each other and hailing them as they passed. The inside of the train was an olive-drab combat zone where the tensions of fear and bravado ground against each other. They were packed in, with all their gear, like cattle; the cars smelled rank from a fog of cigarette smoke and perspiration. They sang First Cavalry songs and more of them than ought to have, bragged.

Crosby's unit was shipped to the front-line trenches along the French border. From a distance, the popping of the rifles had sounded no more harmful than the backfiring of a Model T. But by the end of his first day, the rifles had assumed their own distinctive grunt. A week had passed and there had been no gassing, no death charges. Down the trench, a few men had gotten wounded, but things stayed relatively quiet.

The field between them and the Germans was scorched black from the torches. A few jagged trunks jutted above the flat horizon. The smell of gunpowder hung in acid-smelling yellow clouds above them. Occasionally a black helmet would pop above the trench line, followed by the high-pitched grunt of a rifle. Most of the time the bullet fell short, and he and the boy in the trench next to him, Hambo, joked about the Heinies being worse shots than they were.

Though they hadn't known it when they met, he and Hambo had come from within ten blocks of each other in Brooklyn. After they found that out, it seemed to Crosby that they had made a silent pact to look out for each other. When he would sleep, Hambo would sleep. They'd share their rations and blankets. Their sergeant called them Big Brooklyn and Little Brooklyn. Hambo was tall and looked as though his bones had grown far too much for his skin. You could count his ribs from twenty feet. His cheeks were hollow with little patches of acne cropping up willy-nilly.

Late in their second week, it happened. It came to them first as a faint drone from behind their lines.

"Tanks?" Hambo had asked Crosby. "You think they're bringing up tanks?"

"They didn't tell us about a charge. They're supposed to pass the word."

All the firing stopped on both sides as the drone steadily intensified. Up and down the trenches, bayonets clicked onto the barrels of rifles. Some great and indestructible force was racing from behind them at breakneck speed.

"Oh, Lord," Hambo said. "What's going to happen?" He grabbed Crosby's arm and was squeezing it.

"Say a prayer. We're going to be sandwiched."

Panic electrified the trenches. The ground vibrated like

the beginning of an earthquake. Then in two dark movements above their heads, like shadows of great prehistoric birds, the planes came.

Two of them. So low he could see the pilots' grimacing faces. Their heads were capped in smooth leather; their eyes covered with bulging goggles.

"Those are recon planes," Hambo said. He had not released Crosby's arm and he pumped it excitedly now.

The stutter of the Voison's machine gun cut through the roar of the engines. A bullet tore loose the Fokker's wing strut.

"They're fighting," Hambo said. "Do you see that?"

"I don't believe it," Crosby said.

First the German plane was being chased, then it looped over and nosed in on the tail of the Voison. They circled above the trenches exchanging positions and tearing great slashes through the canvas of each other's fuselages.

The Voison was slower and could not match the maneuverability of the Fokker. Finally, the Fokker shot through the Voison's struts and it started into a topheavy spin. Smoke trailed from behind the cockpit like a gray ribbon. The Fokker chased it down, firing. Before it jammed the ground, the Voison's cockpit erupted in flames, completely engulfing the pilot. Crosby rose out of the trench as the first shock rippled the earth. It came like a hot breath; the heat of the flames seared his face. He stared for an eternity at the stiff silhouette of the pilot outlined against the raging orange flames. He did not think of getting shot; he thought only that he had been touched in some peculiar way by the hot breath of death.

As he came down, Hambo scrambled up. "Don't," Crosby said, but Hambo pulled his leg free of Crosby's grip. There was a single snort, followed by the ting of metal striking metal, and Hambo crumpled to a heap at Crosby's feet. He looked stunned, like someone had knocked the wind out of him, except for the line of blood that split the bridge of his nose and filled his wide eyes. Looking at Hambo, he had felt something inside him snap at that moment, as if he had passed out dizzily, but he had not lost consciousness. He felt his face and chest consumed by infernal heat as though *he* had been the pilot of that burning French plane.

After that single shot, both sides lay still for an hour. The Fokker circled above the German trenches, dipping its wings, but even they did not cheer. It seemed as though they had all sensed the same thing about their lives.

Two days later, in their first charge, he was shot in the knee as he came over the top of the trench. He was sent home in a fog of morphine, tossing with the sight of Hambo's blood-split face and that of the French pilot, tearing at his flaming head.

Crosby slept for nearly two hours, but this talk of Paul's death had triggered the welling up of a lifetime of anxiety that he had worked hard to push out of his head. He understood more of what Owen now faced than he could possibly ever tell. He had outlived so many of his friends that each time now, he wondered if he'd be next, if the numbing would finally overcome him in some paralyzing avalanche. This anxiety had grown like a cyst—it got bigger and more painful, until after Margaret's death, he thought he had it completely excised.

He sat at her desk and laced his brogans. The air in the room had gotten heavier, harder to breathe. He spread back the curtains to let in the afternoon sun, hoping that it would make the room seem larger, his life seem larger too. There was a print of Rembrandt's *Night Watch* that Margaret had hung in a thick gilt frame above the desk. He felt like one of the characters crowded into the darkness behind Captain Banning Cocq, either caught up or about to be caught up in schemes of greatness or madness. It didn't matter. What mattered was the "caught up" part, the inertia against which he was powerless.

Suddenly, the door clicked open. "I'm sorry," Owen said, sticking his head in. "I didn't mean to startle you."

"Did you go off?"

"Yes," he said. "I have to talk with you. I don't know what's going on with me. I feel like I have a fox inside my shirt, gnawing at my belly. I can't scream and I can't get rid of it."

"You sound crazier than a loon." Crosby took a small framed picture of Margaret from the desk. He rolled the top down and walked to the window.

"Where I went was to Paul's house. I told his wife. She called me when I was in his office this morning and asked me to come over."

"What was her reaction?"

"I don't know. She was hurt. She cried, but I don't think she was grief-stricken. I couldn't read her. Maybe it was just a release for her from not knowing."

"Now she knows," Crosby said. The picture in his hand showed Margaret slouching over the arm of a striped chair. A floor lamp beside the chair dully lit her face and shoulders. Her auburn hair was bobbed neatly and a capricious smile radiated from the shadows of her face. It was his favorite picture of her; he even remembered taking it. Now it was the only one he kept.

"I used to be missing all the time with her," he said pathetically. "I'd be gone for weeks sometimes, selling my earthpacking machines. Sometimes I think she'da preferred it if I turned up missing for good. She was a nurse in the Veteran's Hospital where I spent months recuperating after the war. Damned fine looker." He turned from the window and handed Owen the picture of her. "I followed the boom to Florida, working construction, selling corsets. Anything

130

to turn a buck. Sent for her with the first hundred dollars I made on my own."

They sat together on the bed. "She never did like it down here," Crosby said. "All the time complaining about the heat and the bugs. You know what I told her when I proposed to her?"

"What?" Owen had seen that picture of Margaret dozens of times before, but he had never studied it. She was a great beauty, he thought, frail and delicate with thin legs and ankles.

"It was in Palm Beach. In one of those grand hotels. They had ornate balustrades and stairs so high they'd make you dizzy to climb. Crystal chandeliers and murals on the walls the size of this whole house.

"I had a Justice of the Peace waiting up in my room and I took her aside in the lobby and said, 'Margaret, we don't know each other real well. I'm a Presbyterian and I've never had a venereal disease.' "

"You told her that right before you got married?" Owen said, laughing.

"Standing right in the hotel lobby, I did," Crosby said, proudly reaffirming it. "And she said, 'Well, I'm a Catholic.' So I said, 'What about the other part?' She laid a fist across my jaw that sent me flying.

"When I tried to follow her as she ran up the stairs, the bell captain and a couple of his stooges grabbed me and threw me out into the street. Took me three days to get back in that place and I had to sneak at that."

"Did the Justice of the Peace wait?"

"That's not funny."

"Why are you telling me this now?" Owen asked.

"Let's fix us something to eat. You hungry?"

Owen and Crosby went into the kitchen where Crosby took two thick fillets of bass from the refrigerator. He put the fillets in a flat broiling pan, poured lemon juice and melted butter over them, then crushed some oregano between his fingers and sprinkled the fish generously.

Owen sat at the wrought iron kitchenette with the glass top pulling on a Miller and peeling potatoes. "Why didn't you ever remarry?"

"She hated this place. Thought it was a hole in hell, and all those times I shushed her about the heat and the bugs makes me sick. You know it was a snake that got her. Wasn't even a town here then. Just a hole in hell like she said."

"You never told me how she died."

"Wasn't your business."

"I'm sorry."

"Don't be. You asked me why I was telling you all this. I don't know. Might be something in it for you, though I couldn't say what. She blowed up big as a poisoned dog. Her whole leg turned black before I even got home to her." Crosby kept his back to Owen. He busied himself at the sink with the morning's pans and dishes. "I should have stayed with her more. Might not have happened."

"You couldn't have done anything about that. It was her time."

"You can't tell me much about time," he said, taking the sliced potatoes from Owen and dropping them into a deep pan full of hot oil. "She told me, 'Arnold, I'll no sooner be cooled in the ground then you'll be off with some blind whore.' She said that to me right on her death bed. I said, 'A blind whore?' She said, 'She'd have to be blind to go off with a buzzard as ugly as you.'"

Owen wanted to say something to console him, to say he understood, but he didn't understand. He didn't understand anything anymore. Life was just like that.

"I respected her too much is why I didn't tie no more knots," Crosby finally said.

He went into the pantry, and when he came out with a Ball jar full of string beans that he had canned himself, his face had changed from melancholy self-indulgence to a wry puzzled look. His brow was knitted and his eyes held a concentrated piercing stare. He put the beans in the pot and covered them. "Stuff's missing from the pantry."

"I know."

"What you gonna do, boy? No, wait, don't tell me. I don't want to know."

Owen set two places at the table while Crosby removed the bass from the oven. The butter sizzled in the pan as he ran to the table and threw it on the heat pad.

"Whew! That's hot as shit," he said.

"Looks good." Owen took his fork and broke off a hunk of the thick white fillet. He blew it cool and shoved it in his mouth.

"Can't you wait?" Crosby said.

"It's too good." He forked another hunk into his mouth. "Besides, I haven't been eating well lately."

"Nothing's *too* good." Crosby tended the potatoes, then spooned them into a paper-lined dish. "You know there's two things I remember when she died. She was smiling—and God knows to this day I can't figure out why—and her breath was hot enough to melt iron."

That's a heap better than the smell of rubber, Owen thought, and better too than Paul's shocked face as he went under. "You going to the police?"

After a moment, Crosby broke himself off a piece of fish. "Have to," he said.

Owen dropped his fork on his plate. "Shit. Goddamned shit. I'm going to spend the rest of my life in jail. Or dead. But one thing's for sure: I'm not going to make it as old as you. Your beans are boiling."

"I have to do it. Someone has to grab this bull by the balls and I don't give a goddamn about the beans. You wanna talk some more about it?"

"I've been talking and thinking too much lately."

"It's got to end," Crosby said, watching Owen's jaws start to grind together. "If it don't it'll carry over on everything in your life. It's a thing you can't never run away from."

Owen pushed his plate away. "I can't eat," he said.

"You know she took up with Donny?"

"Paul's wife? An affair?"

"Whatever you want to call it."

"How do you know?"

"I saw them. I saw them at Harrah's, that juke out at Prairie Creek. And I saw them swimming buck naked out at his place when I was out on a walk."

Owen remembered the loofah sponges in Donny's bathroom as he tried to find something to clean himself up with. He remembered the cold creams and all the different kinds of shampoos and rinses, but the incongruity of it had not registered with him in the aftershock of Paul's death. It made a perverse kind of sense to him now. He recreated the hard quality of her voice and the strange feeling he had gotten after talking with her. Had she and that fuck planned this thing all along? It was all too bizarre, though no more bizarre than anything else that had gone on these past couple of days.

Sitting in her living room, the house had been filled with her smell. The muted light from the half-open drapes filtered around her as she cried on the couch. He had imagined her as a lover he could never have. And now Crosby was throwing her duplicity on him like a wet rug. He wished he were there now. His thoughts would be less romantic; he'd treat her like the whore she was. Fuck everything else.

The puddle of butter and lemon juice congealed around the fish on his plate. "If she wants any help from me," he said, pushing away from the table, "she can go screw."

"The police are going to come after you, son. Come in with me. I'll see that they treat you right."

"No way. They'll have to catch me. I'm gone."

"They will."

Crosby shouted down the hall after him, "You're gonna make it difficult on yourself."

Owen turned back. "You've got it all wrong. I'm going to make it difficult for everyone else."

Owen changed the dressing over his eye in the bathroom and took the bandage off his left arm altogether. It had healed nicely, leaving only a puckered crescent-shaped red scar. He raised his arm above his head, then circled it to test its movement.

On the phone with Donny, he told him that Crosby was going to the cops to vouch for Lorene's story. He said he'd also been to her house to see her.

"You've really botched things up," Donny said. "You harebrained asshole."

"I hope the cops fuck you good," he said. "And I want money."

"Eat shit," Donny said and slammed the receiver down.

Owen's mind raced with alternatives. He thought of staging something to make the death appear premeditated. Perhaps if he threatened Lorene with the affair, threatened going to the police himself and planting that seed in their minds, he could take the pressure off himself. But too many things weighed against that now. That chance Paul had lectured about, the unbridled fate—the real meat of life—had taken on form and movement and as surely as that abstract of the jaws that hung above Lorene's living room couch, it was snapping at his heels.

CHAPTER

AFTER DONNY AND GEORGIA FINISHED THE BOTTLE OF BUR-gundy he had bought at Buckeye's, she peeled off her jersey. She was standing across from him, in front of the daybed, and she crossed her arms at her waist, then pulled the top over her head in a single fluid movement. Her pert breasts danced as she shook her hair free. Without a word, she dropped her skirt too, and stood before him in the barest suggestion of blue panties.

He undressed too, watching the soft upturned slope of her breasts, trying to see them as he had for the first time.

"Suck them," she said when she saw him staring. She lay back on the bed and rolled her panties down her legs.

He stumbled onto her and began kissing her. Her mouth opened wide and she pushed at his tongue with hers. She ground against him hungrily; it was just what he needed.

She consumed his tongue and he felt for an instant that she had consumed him too, in his entirety. He had slipped through to the other side of thought. Her mouth tasted of wine and cigarettes; she squirmed underneath him, raking his back with her long brown-painted nails. He rolled both her hard nipples in his teeth.

"Do it to me," she said. "Do it to me now."

When the phone rang, he started to pull out of her but she caught him. Her face was flushed, contorted, as though she had been coming all along. She bit her brown lips. "No," she said. "Stay."

He tried pulling away again and she dug her talons into his back sharply. It stopped ringing.

He made love to her a long time after that. The nagging curiosity of the phone call, and his intuition that he should have answered it, carried him away from the intense feeling in his cock till it was nothing more than a numb stroking, and he could not bring himself off.

Afterwards, she said, "You're some kind of great fuck."

He wiped the beads of perspiration from her forehead and she wrapped her arms and legs around him. All bones, he thought. Not like Fauna. His own sweat drenched the sheets under him and he rolled her off him.

"What are you going to tell him this time?" he asked her. Their faces were only inches apart. He could feel her breath on his chest. Her black eyes narrowed.

"It's nothing to you what I tell him." She turned her back to him and pulled the sheet up. Her shoulder blades folded back along her spine like a pair of wings.

"I didn't mean it," he said, kissing along the knuckles of her backbone. When he had first started making it with her, he wondered what she had told her husband, and if she had ever gone from his place to her husband's bed. Once, she had told him that her husband had asked what the wad of toilet paper was doing in her panties when she undressed for the night. She said it was for discharge, and Donny suspected that her husband was more stupid than she.

"I thought doing this would help," he finally said.

"Help what?" Georgia kept her face turned to the wall. She was pouting now and he didn't have the patience to draw her out.

"The tension, you know, the campaign. Oh, never mind." The grumble of machines at the mine carried on the air to him now. They must have started up while he was distracted with his lovemaking and he wondered who in the hell was running this conspiracy to drive him nuts. "Want a beer?"

"I'll have some of yours," she said. "I'm looped as it is."

When he came back, she had combed out her tangle of long black hair and was sitting on the bed in a lotus position. Her back was straight and her nipples angled up to the ceiling. She was looking out the screen, above the half-wall. "Did you buy a new boat?"

"No," he said. He turned the rocker away from the screen and propped his feet on the bed. The wall behind her was green and the paleness of her skin, with her black hair and deep-set black eyes made her look like the statue of an Indian goddess.

"Where did you get it?"

"Forget about it," he said, handing her a half-filled glass while he sipped at the can.

"My momma used to stay drunk all the time on this kind of beer," she said, nodding to the Pabst can in Donny's hand. "Many's the time I was called away from school to fetch her out of trouble."

"She have black eyes too?"

"Her eyes were blacker. So black I was scared to look into them if she was drunk."

Donny took one of her cigarettes from his desk and lit it.

"When did you take up smoking?"

"Right now," he said. The smoke burned his throat, and he thought if there had been heroin on the table beside him, he would have taken that up too. "Was your daddy a drunk too?"

"Why are you talking to me like this?" she said, shoving the glass at him. "Didn't I do it good for you? My daddy was a chief and the mayor of Cherokee, North Carolina and you're a sonofabitch."

"I don't know what's gotten into me," he said. "It's nothing you've done. I didn't mean it to be this way."

He wanted to talk with her as he had talked with Fauna as they lay in each other's arms. He needed her to tell him things he could not know. But he couldn't get it out right. He needed to hear her tell him how strong he was, that he was not a bad man. He needed that anchor to keep him from drifting into the nightmares he was having day and night. Fauna had told him that he was her counterweight that balanced what was missing in her relationship with Paul and kept her from truly hating his weaknesses. Well, he needed a counterweight now, goddamnit, or he'd flip right into that world of blank stares, bathrobes and slippers.

Donny watched as the light changed over the lake. There was a cool that settled when the sun sank below the pines. It awakened the darker tones in all the vibrant greens and yellows of the afternoon, and now it washed over him, and Georgia who lay curled into the pillow on the bed beside him.

When the phone rang, Donny leapt out of the chair and answered it. "Did you call before?"

"No," Owen said.

"Well, somebody did. Your stupidity is costing me everything in the world. Now Crosby's in this . . ."

"I haven't cost you anything," Owen interrupted. "Yet. You brought all this on yourself and you dragged me into it. I want money."

"For what?"

"To get the hell out of here."

"It's all tied up in the campaign. I can't get any."

"That's bullshit. If I'm caught, you're caught. They'll deal with me to talk against you. I'm small potatoes."

"You watch too many television shows."

"Five thousand."

"What do you think, I keep that kind of money laying around? Where can I get in touch with you?"

"I won't say. I don't want anybody to know anything about me. When Crosby spills it, there's going to be a shitload of trouble. I want you to know," Owen said, "this isn't blackmail. I *have* to leave."

"A rose by any other name. How can I reach you?"

"You can't." Owen hung up and a panic, like a pair of hands, tightened Donny's throat.

□ □

The first time Donny encountered Crosby, he had been addressing the Putnam Chapter of the National Wildlife Organization in the basement of the First Baptist Church. The basement was thick with the smell of oiled wooden pews, smoke, and the collective musk of Putnam's outdoorsmen. Donny had recruited most of them personally from the hunting and bass clubs. They were simpleminded men who only responded when he could show them that ecological destruction in a remote area could directly affect their hunting and fishing.

As he read aloud the newest study on the status of the Great Bald Eagle, he tried to tie their diminishing numbers to the shrinking game and fish stocks. They were an accurate barometer of ecosystem destruction, he had said. When he got to the point where he was showing the active and productive nesting sites on a chart his secretary drew, a voice

140

came from the back of the room. It was deep and clear and it stopped him in mid-sentence.

"That report's a lot of horseshit."

It stunned him. The faces he held mesmerized in front of him, all in neat rows with their woodsmen shirts and denim jackets rolled at the wrist, all of them, turned in unison. "What?" he said. "Who said that?"

"I did," the voice answered. An old man stood from a seat in the rear of the room. "I said it's horseshit because I know the people that put it together and they wouldn't know an eagle if it bit them on the ass." The meeting cracked up. Catcalls came from the back, and one of the men in the front —MacPherson—shrilled like a siren.

"I think this report's an excellent update on the research available," Donny countered, but the room hadn't settled yet. He wanted to punch out that old fuck.

"The eagle's not in near as bad shape as you been saying. There's three sites you got marked on that chart that don't exist anymore. And at least half a dozen more I know about that are a spitting distance from that cluster in the left-hand corner. Crosby's the name," the old man said. "And I didn't mean to take the steam out of your presentation, but I know for a fact that that report is either falsified or in error."

"Those are pretty serious allegations, Mr. Crosby. Why would it be falsified?"

"State funding's one reason. And you don't have to be so serious, Mr. Waldo."

"You're disputing some very accurate findings. The Fish and Game Commission is a reputable group . . ."

"It's only as reputable as each man on it. There's sons of bitches and damn fine fellows and I suspect the former prepared what you got pressed up against your chest."

MacPherson whistled again and it caught like an epidemic. Soon the whole room was in an uproar. Donny had brought the report closer to him as Crosby talked. He gripped the binding tighter, as though he could shield himself from that cantankerous old asshole.

"I have a whole album of pictures out in my truck if you'd like me to *substantiate* what I just said," Crosby said, his tone changing. "I'm really not looking for an argument, Mr. Waldo. These meetings usually end up being places where people flap their jaws and don't do shit about nothing but get drunk in the parking lot after, and I figured since we got us a lawyer now, we might could just get heard for once."

Donny poured himself a glass of water from the pitcher on the table in front of him. "Well, I appreciate your candor, sir."

After the meeting, Donny caught Crosby outside as he was getting into his truck. The truth in what the old man said surfaced through his instant loathing of him. Though his tone had been arrogant, he could see in the mild clarity of his eyes, sunk deep in stretched shiny cheeks, that he believed what he said. And for that instant, Donny believed too.

"Jeez," he said as Crosby unlocked his truck, "you had everybody in there shook up. Me included." Donny extended Crosby his hand.

"Wasn't my intention," Crosby said meekly. "I really didn't mean to steal your thunder."

"Don't worry about it. Listen, could you show me some of those nests you were talking about?"

"Maybe," Crosby said, getting into the cab. He rolled down the window. "Call me."

Two months later, they arranged to meet at the Prairie Creek Boat Ramp before dawn. It was a graveled turn-off from Highway 20 where the Negroes fished for catfish and carp. Cypress trees twined out of the moist dark dirt, out of the water itself, like strands of gray muscle straining to smooth out against the pale dawn sky. On the other side of the road, osprey nests topped the silhouettes of dead, denuded trees like clumps of wild hair.

Crosby had already started removing the canoe from the back of his truck when Donny came bouncing around the bend and onto the turnoff. He popped out of his car. "Hold on and let me give you a hand with that."

"I've done it alone before," Crosby said, tugging the stern of the canoe.

Donny hadn't seen him since the meeting, but he thought of him constantly—that arrogant voice, the far-off icy glare of his eyes. He didn't know whether to love him or hate him for the embarrassment he had caused. And he was wearing the exact same outfit, as if to further remind him of his humiliation: a faded checkered shirt buttoned at the wrists; baggy khaki trousers; and a sweat-stained, battered straw hat.

He helped Crosby slide the canoe the rest of the way out and they carried it to the bank. Donny loaded a small styrofoam cooler and Crosby stowed his camera gear and a brown paper sack.

The silence along the creek was stunning. It made Donny giddy. He could even hear the tinkle of the canoe's wake as it curled onto the glassy surface of the water. "This is absolutely beautiful," he said. He wanted to tell Crosby, right then, about his idea for the Group, how they might do great things, but Crosby seemed perturbed about life in general, and he decided to wait until the right time.

The creek wound for three miles, and maneuvering through one of the many bends, they disturbed a great blue heron fishing in the lily pads. It stood three feet high with a wingspan nearly as wide as the creek itself; and as it pumped away downstream, it startled Donny. He saw a gator too, lying still in the water like a black log. It disappeared in an insuck of bubbles as they approached. He thought Crosby could teach him many things about the outdoors.

All he had to do was get rid of his intense dislike for the man's terseness.

They beached at a clearing that opened onto Newnan's Lake. Crosby told him to gather as much morning glory vines as he could and they draped the tripods, the camera and the telescope.

"I've set for days and not got a single shot. Don't get your hopes too high."

Crosby carefully focused each instrument on the eyrie. "I'ye been trying for *this* here shot for six months," he continued. He attached an 800-mm. lens. "Here, take a look."

"That's the eyrie?" Donny squinted hard and all he saw was a thick pine branch.

"What'd you expect? A condominium? Look real close and you'll see where the bark's worn away."

"Yeah," Donny said. "I see it." In the middle of the branch, the bark had been worn through, showing speckles of white pine underneath.

"This particular eagle may wear that branch clear through." Crosby laughed to himself, then wheezed. "Lemme see those binoculars."

Donny retrieved them from the canoe and Crosby stood behind their elaborate wall of camouflage and focused downstream where the mouth of the creek opened onto the huge lake.

He gave Donny the glasses. "He's still preening. Look up the clump of six cypress, and above it, under the canopy of that slash pine, you'll see something that wasn't in your status report."

Donny scanned the trees on the nipple of land that stuck out into the lake. Each limb blended with another and he could not understand how Crosby could pick anything out in that tangle of green and gray. Finally, in the dim shadows of the pine's umbrella, he saw their small white heads. "How old?" he asked.

"Six, maybe seven."

"Looks like a fortress," Donny said, dropping his arms. The nest was a gnarl of twigs and small branches woven thick as a three-hundred-pound bale of hay and nestled into the underside of the pine's bushy crown.

"It ought to. They build on it every year. Keep your eye on it for a while. When you see one of 'em lift off, we're in business."

Donny propped himself against a wild plum tree while Crosby cleaned his lenses and loaded his camera. They passed a pitcher of tea between them and Crosby palmed a fistful of chewing tobacco into his mouth.

"Your report said that light planes were the chief means of spotting. Remember?"

"So?"

"A plane passing over that nest would miss it." He adjusted his straw hat and spit a stream of juice into the dirt beside him.

"I've been toying with an idea for a long time now," Donny said. "Wanna hear it?"

"All right."

"I want to form a group that would splinter away from the Wildlife Organization. All we ever do at those meetings is get mired down with bullshit about what the state chapter is doing and what the legislature isn't doing. You and I could . . ."

Crosby interrupted him. "I don't have time to fool with causes. I'm eighty-three."

"No, it's nothing like that." Donny kept watching the nest through the binoculars as he talked. "Any immatures?"

"One, I think."

"A group of people like us," he continued. "We could monitor them. Present our findings. This would be a chance to do something. Like you said at the meeting."

"Sounds like a waste of time to me." Crosby worked his

way to his feet. "You want lunch now?" He dug a hole in the sandy ground with a single thrust of his heel, then dropped the wad of tobacco in and covered it.

Donny spread his lunch on top of the cooler and sat facing Crosby, who said he'd watch the nest for a while.

"Want a piece of chicken?" Donny tore into a crisp breast.

"Too wet."

"The chicken?"

"No. The ground. The air. Those birds might dry their wings all day. I brought my own lunch."

Crosby ate a hard-boiled egg with salt and washed it down with tea from his own canteen.

"I know of a group of eagle-lovers up in New York. Real patriots. The Eagle Command. I believe they're a splinter group from the Birchers."

"That's not what I had in mind," Donny said, "and you know it. Why don't you cut me a little slack. You're ornery as a bitch in heat."

"Humor an old man." Crosby pointed toward the nest. "There's a movement."

Donny sprang to his feet. Crosby pushed over on his knees and worked himself up the sweetgum tree he sat beside.

The eagle lifted from the nest, gliding above the treetops.

"It's the daddy," Crosby said, adjusting the lens of his camera. "Take the telescope."

They hunched over their equipment. The eagle's long wings almost touched the treetops on the downsweep; then he caught a rise and began to soar, drifting over the lake in slow deliberate spirals. Each circle moved upward into the next smaller one till the detail of his striking white head and tail blended with the deep brown of his body. He floated higher still, and then, as though he had something else to do, he began a sharp controlled descent.

"He's going for the eyrie," Crosby said.

"How do you know?"

146

"His wings wouldn't dry, I bet. And he has to hunt from somewhere."

"Shit," Donny exclaimed. "This is exciting." His voice sounded to him as it had when he was a child. He felt a line of gooseflesh prickle the nape of his neck.

"No more talking," Crosby said.

The eagle grew gradually larger in Donny's lens. He could see the power of the sweeping wings, feel it as they beat the air. He felt an awful reverence for the bird, and decided right then that he would form the Group with or without Crosby's help.

The eagle lit on the branch—in the exact spot that Crosby had pointed out to him earlier. As the armored talons tightened around the limb, he could feel the intensity of their grip inside his belly.

"He'll do his hunting from there today," Crosby said. He began working the shutter of his camera madly, snapping off picture after picture.

"Can he hear that?" The click of the camera seemed like the only sound in the woods to Donny.

"If you'll put your face back in the telescope, you'll have your answer."

The eagle stared straight at them. The scruff of the white fur-like feathers above his bony brow made him look incensed; his large yellow eyes held a mixture of contempt and curiosity. He bobbed and weaved, then shifted from one leg to the other.

"He's heard us," Donny said.

"Seen," Crosby corrected. "He's seen us." Without stopping his picture-taking, he said, "His vision is hundreds of times better than ours. Has to be. Flying through dense forest at sixty miles per hour, if he so much as nicks a branch, it'd tear his wing off."

"But we're three hundred yards away."

"Probably coulda seen us if we were two miles away."

"Jesus," Donny said with some piety.

"An eagle with a busted wing ain't majestic at all. It's just another dead bird. See what's going on at the nest."

Donny drew the nest into focus. "I can see some gray fur now. Must be the chick. And there," he said, "wouldya look at that."

Crosby shifted his camera from the eyrie to the nest. "Well, what do you know. The momma." She had her head pressed low into the side of the nest so that only the sharp curve of her yellow beak and the wild tuft of her brow showed.

"Something's up," Crosby said. "She's watching something."

Just then, a red-tailed hawk streaked low into the cypress trees, landing under the nest on a branch she couldn't see. He and Donny wouldn't have seen the hawk at all, but as quickly as it had become a movement inside her territory, she released a terrifying scream.

The woods became silent, except for the metronomic ticking of a distant woodpecker. And then there was the answer, an equally alarming and sustained scream that carried through the woods faster than wind. Crosby picked up Donny's binoculars just as the male shot away from his eyrie. Crosby followed him as he swept the pearlescent midday sky behind him at treetop level. "So fast," was all he could say. He wanted to slow down time, to watch the muscles of his underside expand and contract with each pendulous pump of his wings.

"Quick, get on the camera," Donny said.

Crosby threw the binoculars aside, screwed the lens on and focused on the hawk, who sat oblivious on the cypress branch.

When the eagle was a hundred feet away, the hawk took off. He had just crested the trees when they heard another scream. At full speed, the charging eagle pulled in his wings and curled forward, hitting the hawk in mid-beat with the accumulated force of his beak and opened talons.

"Like a bullet," Crosby said.

"Did you see that?" Donny yelled. "It exploded. The fuckin' hawk exploded." He turned to Crosby, who was beaming like a kid with a candy bar.

"Not only did I see it, but I think I got it all, right here on film."

When they had packed up their gear and stowed it neatly in the canoe, Crosby said, "When are you holding your Group's first meeting?"

"You gonna come?"

"Might."

□   □

The only people that the Group's first meeting brought together were Donny, Crosby, Paul McGavin, and the Mayberry brothers—a pair of identical twin farmers in VFW caps with flag pins in their lapels who came because they thought it was going to be a patriotic organization.

Donny had convinced Crosby to hold the first meeting at his house. Set an acre in from Lake Cayuka, it was a high-roofed clapboard house with a screened porch three-quarters of the way around. Inside, the walls were dark-stained pine board. Two pale green, imitation Louis XIV love seats faced each other in front of a large brick fireplace. Renaissance prints hung in gold frames above the mantel.

Crosby stayed behind the bar the whole afternoon, fixing drinks for everyone except himself. The Mayberry brothers looked older than Crosby by ten years. Their eyes were nearly puffed closed from the fat of their cheeks; each had a birthmark the size of a quarter, an inch below their eyeglasses, so that they looked like a perfect set of bookends in every way. They argued first about the Group's motto and emblem; they wanted an eagle wrestling with a snake in a red, white and blue tree. Underneath, it would say: Don't Tread on Me (or Us—they couldn't decide on the diction).

Donny countered their arguments for nearly a half hour before he realized they were insane. Paul lay on the floor in front of the fireplace, drinking Scotch and soda and giggling at Donny and the Mayberry brothers.

When they had gotten drunk enough, the Mayberry brothers shut up and sat sullenly in the love seats facing Crosby at the bar.

Donny tried talking about what he and Crosby had seen out on Prairie Creek in a meaningful way, but Paul had gotten too drunk to appreciate it. And the Mayberry brothers could not seem to equate what he was saying with the olive branch and the arrows.

Finally, Paul said, "That certainly was dramatic. Crosby, fix me another Scotch, will ya?" The Mayberry brothers left belching. Nobody told them where the next meeting was to be held.

□   □

When Owen had walked out of the kitchen, Crosby was left to stare at the food on his plate. He could not eat alone, and it appeared as though Owen was gone for good. When he had seen the food missing from the pantry, the walls closed on him. It was as though his own kin had stolen from him, though he knew that that was not the case. He would have given him anything, helped him in any way, but the kid had started his own inertia and he would have to live with it.

He scraped the fish, potatoes and beans into a plastic bucket that he kept under the sink and carried it out to the compost heap by the chicken coop. Then he left for town.

150

Crosby knew that going to Putnam Hall's sheriff wouldn't accomplish anything. He was a rotund, stupid man who had a star painted on the side of his Oldsmobile 442. The sweat stains in the puckers of his khaki shirt looked like Rorschach tests; and he could deal with nothing more sophisticated than the Saturday night drunks at Buckeye's.

The police station was situated between the old railroad freight yard and the edge of the ghetto. It was a white two-story building. The side was painted with day-glo murals of a skyline that didn't exist, punctuated by palmetto trees. Television was responsible for this, Crosby thought, as he pulled into the parking lot beside a fleet of black-and-whites. He locked the truck before he went in.

After he told the desk sergeant that he wanted to report a homicide, he was escorted into a soundproofed room by a matronly policewoman who acted as casual as if he were reporting a stolen social security check.

"Detective Fletcher will be right with you," she said. "Make yourself comfortable." She closed the door behind him and he felt like he had just walked into a trap. The door did not have an inside handle. The only furniture in the room was a metal table, bolted to the floor, and three straightbacked metal chairs.

An eternity passed before the door opened and the detective came in. Crosby said, "Let me tell you my story and get out of here. I don't like this place."

"Take it easy, Mr. Crosby," the detective said, easing him back down into his chair. "Homicide is no small matter. My name is Fletcher." He reached out and shook Crosby's hand. He wore a blond moustache on a child's face. His cheeks were mottled pink; his eyes were crisp blue with flecks of brown in one, and green in the other. He had one of those new hairdos that looked chopped-up but somehow orderly.

"I don't really know if it was homicide or not. I just said that to get some attention. All I know's somebody's been killed and nothing's being done about it."

Crosby told him Owen's story, and Fletcher said, "We've been in contact with Mrs. McGavin. Do you know where this Brown kid is now?"

"He left my place about an hour before I came here."

"We'll have to pick him up. Where was he going?"

"I don't know. He didn't say and I didn't ask. What about Donny Waldo?"

"Waldo's not going anywhere. I'd like to gather everybody and have a little shindig, so to speak." Fletcher picked at his cuticles with a bent paper clip, alternately looking at Crosby, then his fingers. "Waldo's the last one I want to invite."

"Why don't you find Paul's body first?"

"I don't have the authority to free the entire force from their regular duties to search those pits, and that's about what it would take. There are more mines out there than trees. If you could have told me where to look . . ."

"He didn't tell me," Crosby interrupted.

"Then we need the kid."

□   □

It was well past dusk when Crosby left the police department and drove east out Highway 20 toward Putnam Hall. The pink line of sky behind him was dulling under the wash of purple night. He wished that he had never consented to Donny's idea for the Group. He felt somehow responsible for the shape of things now. There was no end to this inertia that started in his youth. Now it seemed as though Owen had stepped into its path and was caught up in it.

He could not understand why the cops wouldn't pull

Donny in. Some grand melodrama was being choreographed; and he was somebody's chess piece, though he couldn't figure out whose. He was too old for this sort of intrigue; it pulled at him from the inside, tiring him. Since Owen had told him, there had been a constant tremble in his chest. At first it alarmed him, but he gradually calmed to it. And driving home along the unlit two-lane blacktop, the amber flashers confusing him with detours, it had come back again, only stronger. He could feel his pulse hopping in his neck.

A set of bright lights, blinding and set low to the ground, rounded one of the curves coming out of a detour and edged him onto the shoulder of the road. Sonofabitch bastard, Crosby thought. The words felt good. He looked in his rear-view mirror at the taillights growing smaller. "Sonofabitch bastard," he said again.

He had not liked Donny from that first instant. He always knew that Donny wanted something from him, and from anyone he dealt with. You always went away feeling like something had been sucked out of you after spending time with him. It wasn't until the day he caught him lying about that eagle story, that he could hang his dislike on a peg. He had known he was a liar all along, but it had taken him more than a year to name it.

When Crosby got home, he fixed a dish of cottage cheese with fresh pear sliced into it. Eating it on the porch, he stared at the monstrous silhouette of a live oak that spread over nearly half an acre of his front lawn. Some of the limbs stretched for a hundred feet, and in the light of the full moon, they looked like the thick reaching tendrils of an octopus.

He tried reading the paper in bed before going to sleep, but there were so many VOTE DONALD "DONNY" WALDO paid political advertisements that it made him sick. He threw the paper on the floor, turned out his lamp, and patted the

153

bedspread around him so that it hugged the outline of his body. UNBOUGHT—INDEPENDENT—PEOPLE-ORIENTED, the ads said. Hogwash.

□　□

Donny left Georgia sleeping in the daybed; he got into his midnight blue MG and drove to town for his Lions Club speech. It was the winding down now of the campaign and the press was supposed to be there to get his final statement before the voting booths opened in the morning.

After working through the gears, the steady drone of the engine and the hypnotic flashing of the white divider lines lulled him into a dreamy somnolence. His arms spanned heavily away from his chest; his hands worked the steering wheel of their own accord. He had become a mechanism—an inextricable part—of this humming capsule as it raced through the dusk.

He had shaved with mind-shattering patience after sleeping with Georgia. He felt the pull of each hair as it gave way to the blade. Then he dressed; each thing in its own time. He needed to distract himself constantly now. Whenever he let go, thought for an instant of Paul's smooth, plastic skin as he swiped the sand away, or the weight on his shoulders—the weight of the world—as he carried him to the edge, his insides rumbled a warning of some godawful explosion that would rend him, flesh and blood and guts, into oblivion.

In distraction, there is sanity, he thought. Then: I'm not a bad man. No, not a bad man. The curves came fast, unexpected. The engine's vibration shot up through the accelerator, along his leg to the base of his spine like a constant electric shock. He felt the bow of the boat rising higher and he floored the accelerator to push it down. He was afraid that if he looked in the mirror he would see Paul, bouncing wildly along the road at the end of the ski rope.

He had nearly run some fuck off the road on a curve he wasn't sure he was going to make. When he saw that the truck had recovered, he pressed his accelerator to the floor and vanished.

At the Holiday Inn, a valet in a purple vest and black pants took his car. Another similarly dressed man ushered him inside to meet the Lions' president. There was a circle of purple and yellow all around him; purple and yellow flags with golden L's in the center hung from every wall in the dining hall. Billowing clouds of cigar smoke collided high against the ceiling and he expected to hear the crack of thunder at any second. They sat him at the head of the banquet table.

Favor-seekers on either side distracted him. It was the first time he had ever felt courted; it made him feel important. He picked at his rare roast beef and Yorkshire pudding. All the time, he sensed their eyes on him. He could taste their envy in the meat and gravy. Some of them would draw their heads together, then shoot a glance his way all at the same moment, as though they were reaffirming something in themselves through his presence.

After dinner, the president—a ruddy-faced man with a bellowing voice—introduced him as the next Congressman to the U. S. House of Representatives, even though they all knew he was running for the state legislature.

"Thank you, Mr. President," Donny said, approaching the podium, "but Washington has too many rats' nests for me. I'd like to stay right here in Florida where I can do some real good."

The president led the applause, raising his hands high above his head as if to signal everyone to join in. The irony of his remark brought a sharp pain to Donny's side. There was not a thing that he could say to these people that would not be a lie now. There was not a single piece of his world that was still intact. He was no longer fighting his high-principled battle. That had been shattered with the roar of Owen's engine. He was fighting now to stay alive.

"Washington," Donny exclaimed above their din, "had no idea what the barge canal was doing to the state until a bunch of Florida boys stood up and said, 'Hey, now. Hold on. Let's take us a real close look at this wolf in sheep's clothing.'

"No, gentlemen, the power is not in Washington. It's right here. With you businessmen who want to bring new industry and economic growth to our state without the wholesale destruction of the only legacy we have—our precious land.

"And power is with you farmers too, who are sick and tired of being paid while your plows lie idle. It's people like you and me that have to deal with the real problems of day-to-day living and not the paper-shufflers that keep this country in the muck it's in."

Before he finished, he went through his entire platform—civic responsibility, rising crime, the death penalty, the draining of prairies and wetlands. Afterwards, they questioned him. About broadening the tax base and bussing, about rezoning and Arabs buying beachfront property. His mouth clicked off answers automatically, as though it could run on its own forever now.

The press had been let in and they repeated the same questions. It all seemed rehearsed, calculated to aggravate his senses. Donny's answers moved through his lips like a tape playing back. They crowded around him; their faces stretched into oblong masks. Some vague part of his consciousness drew him out of his body and away from the hustle. He could see the crowd around him from a marvelous distance—like he was looking through one of those convex mirrors in a

Seven-Eleven. He saw himself there too, at the center of the crowd and doing a superb job with them. Words formed sentences and popped like bubbles from his lips. Occasionally the men laughed.

And from that convex, brightly reflective vision, he saw the truck again, running off the road. It was a streak of uncontrolled lights coming at him. Then as he watched the taillights right themselves for this second time, they became framed in his mind, a photo in the chrome of his rearview mirror. Owen's warning. Crosby was coming from the cops; it was *his* testimony that would do him in. Not Owen's. Owen wanted out. The realization burned into his brain— the fucking old bastard. The world was out to destroy him. People were finally starting to take the licks that would cost him his life. His vision of the high-ceilinged, smoke-filled room, of the close musky pressing of the crowd around him, suddenly became reduced to an electrical tingle that grew in intensity till it screamed inside his veins.

When Donny cut his headlights and coasted off Blanding Road into Crosby's driveway, it was eleven-thirty. His front wheels slid through a buffer of thick sand, then bounced in the ruts. Branches scraped the side of his car like steel wire. He parked under one of the outstretched limbs of a single huge live oak that stood on Crosby's lawn.

Crosby's pickup was parked by the porch. Except for the bright aura of light that emanated in waves from the moon, the sky was purple and crowded with stars. As he approached the porch, he felt the hood of the truck. The engine had cooled. He went around to the side window, slid it up and slipped through into the living room. The light entering the windows bathed the room in silver. Sidestepping the shadows of furniture, Donny found himself propped against the hallway wall, breathing heavily.

What the fuck am I doing here, he thought. What could I have ever possibly planned? His mind felt like it had snapped. It was a reeling image on a television screen that had suddenly righted itself. His spine turned to water as he realized that he hadn't been conscious of anything since those reporters had started asking him questions. Not of leaving the banquet, nor of driving, nor even of climbing through the window. He had been pulled along the unlighted highway by some force more powerful than himself and it had taken shape in the form of those taillights. His insanity had become palpable to him now as the pounding of his own heart inside his chest.

The springs on Crosby's bed creaked. Donny heard the faint rustle of covers, then the old man's feet padding across the uncarpeted floor. He wanted to get out of there and at the same time, he wanted to run in and hug Crosby. He wanted to make him see what a mess he had gotten into. He needed help; everything had gotten too far out of hand.

He heard a drawer slide open. All he could think of was gun. Crosby was going for a gun. He moved quickly along the wall to the bedroom. He needed to get there without startling him. He needed to make him see *his* truth. It was the only thing that mattered now.

Crosby's silhouette filled the door frame; silver light filtered all around him. Donny practically bumped into him.

"Who are you?" Crosby asked, raising both white arms. He pointed at Donny with both hands clasped. "What are you doing in my house?"

Donny said, "Can I expl . . ."

There was the sound of a hammer clicking.

"Noo," Donny yelled as he lunged at the shadow. The gun broke away from Crosby's hands like a piece of clay. He rode him backwards until he was on top of him on the bed. The old man's gasping, like a pumping bellows, filled the entire room. Crosby grabbed at his chest, then pounded it.

"My God, is it your heart?" Donny said.

The whole room pulsed with labored breathing; it seemed

intensely hot. Crosby gripped Donny's thigh with his right hand and held it tight.

"I'm sorry," Donny said. He kneaded and pounded the flaccid skin of Crosby's chest with the palms of his hands. "I wasn't . . . I wanted to explain. That's all I was doing here. It's the truth."

Crosby's eyes glowed like cinders in the darkness. His head twitched spasmodically against the rumple of white covers.

"Come on," Donny whispered. "Don't die."

With a shrill whistle, Crosby let out his last breath and the room fell dead. Crosby's hand slid from Donny's knee. "No," Donny cried. "Not now. Not again."

After a moment, he straightened the sheets and covered Crosby as though he were sleeping. He cursed the part of himself that reminded him that he was getting good at cleaning up after his victims. He found the gun on the floor and disengaged the hammer. He shoved it into his pants.

In the living room, he dusted the window clean of his prints. He turned on the television and sat in the love seat and watched the test pattern. The only thing he felt through the numbness at his very center was the hard steel in the waistband of his pants. He was stretched infinitely in all directions. He had to make a conscious effort to blink. He took out the gun and put the barrel in his mouth. The metal was cold as snow on his lips. He wanted to pull the trigger, taste the warm sulfur of his own blood running over his tongue. He wanted to rend himself flesh and blood and guts into oblivion. Finally, he shut off the set and left through the same window he had come in by.

CHAPTER

OWEN STOPPED BY LORENE'S HOUSE EARLY TUESDAY MORNING.
He knew Crosby had been to the cops—the old man seldom
broke his word—and he knew too they'd be after him now.
He parked his van in a shopping center parking lot and
waited in an alley for three-quarters of an hour for a white
Plymouth with a man in a dark suit sitting in it to leave.
Then he hopped the McGavins' fence and came around the
front of the house and knocked.

"What are you doing here?" she asked immediately.
"Don't you know they're watching this place?" She took him
by the arm and pulled him in.

He wanted to ask her why the sudden concern, why the
change. It was not what was called for in her game plan
and would only prolong things. She had made it painfully
clear to him that she wanted anything but that. All he could
say was, "You look terrible. What happened?"

Her hair, which had been so finely put into place the day before, was now a shock of uncombed straw. She was wrapped in a brown floor-length bathrobe that had a delicate white lace trimming the collar. Her long smooth neck and face were pale; her eyes were circled underneath with crescents of gray. Stain from wearing makeup, he thought, like the tannic stain of coffee in a cheap porcelain cup.

"You don't look too good yourself. Where did you sleep last night?"

"In the woods," he said. "I'm out of Crosby's."

She ushered him into the living room. The drapes were drawn and the chromium lamp bowing out of the corner from a single wire gave off a small concentrated island of light. "You want coffee? Breakfast?"

"Coffee's fine."

From the couch, he could see her moving about awkwardly through the kitchen, clanking the coffee pot on the faucet as she filled it. She had cursed once, and from her frantic movements he thought she must have spilled some of the grounds.

"I haven't slept," she said. "They've been out there all night. I don't know what's going on. I suppose it's you they want."

There was a blanket balled in the corner of the couch. A half-empty tumbler of brandy sat beside an open pill vial on the coffee table and magazines were scattered on the floor.

She popped her head out of the kitchen and said, "It'll take a few minutes now. I'm going to freshen up."

He stretched back on the couch and closed his eyes. He had not slept well in the van. The softness of the couch with its smooth velvet-like upholstery caressed his back. He had left his sleeping bag out on the river, and had woken up repeatedly during the night from the chill and dampness.

The place he had stayed was a poor choice. He had driven

out Crosby's drive and down the winding clay road till it ended in the old Florida settlement of Cousin Town. The weathered raw pine cabins had long since been abandoned. With their rusted, corrugated tin roofs, they looked like a picture postcard setting out of early Americana. Behind this row of half a dozen cabins there stretched a lush green pasture—freshly limed—and bordered by a treeline of live oaks, pines, cabbage palms, and palmettos. The vegetation was its own best contrast, with the pine and oak reaching their southernmost limit, while the palms reached their northernmost. Crosby had called it an Eden because the vegetation brought with it the best wildlife of both the north and the south.

At Cousin Town, there had been one of the great battles of the Seminole War. There were markers in the cemetery —grown weedy—of soldiers who had come from as far north as Illinois, Indiana, and Massachusetts in pursuit of some grand conquest. They had followed Jackson in from Palatka where they met the moccasins, the gators and the Indians. And now their bones were dissolved in the limestone, and the markers that proclaimed what they came for—God's Greater Glory, One Union—were crumbling away.

What made the choice a poor one was the cemetery. Behind it, Owen had stashed Crosby's boat till he could come back and get it before heading out to the river. The terrible ironies of the cemetery and the boat, and Paul, and everything that had been happening since Sunday kept him from falling soundly to sleep.

He had stripped several cabbage palms nearly bare of fronds to cover the boat. The whole time he promised himself that he would leave Crosby a note as to where he could pick it up. If he ever got out of this, he would never so much as look at a boat for the rest of his life.

When darkness finally came, he had nothing to do but

sit through the agony that he knew was coming, until he passed out from exhaustion.

For hours he jumped at each crack of a twig in the darkness, expecting the floodlights to come on, followed by the bullhorns. "Give it up, kid. You're surrounded." With time, he convinced himself that only happened on television. He wondered if Lorene weren't somehow mixed up in a conspiracy with Donny. Though it was crazy, it was not too crazy. After all, if anyone had told him that he would spend the rest of his life running from an accomplice to murder charge, he would have thought them crazy. The running part was believable enough. He had resigned himself to that. But the content of his fear, the content of that which kept him running, had always been something that had come from inside him. It was something he manufactured. And because he manufactured it, he always knew he could find a way out. But now, it was in the hands of others, who took a somewhat less than kindly view of his situation. What he was running from now had a penalty attached. Confinement. Suffocation. His hands shook at the thought of it.

In the bedroom, Lorene sat at the vanity and with tissue and cold cream wiped under her eyes and applied fresh eye shadow. The pale blue powder brought out the speckles of darker green in her eyes. She brushed rouge high on her cheekbones, then smoothed out her hair and piled it on top of her head.

She was glad Owen was out there. He was the only link she had with Paul, and through Paul, in some insane way, with Sara Halfacre who had constantly reappeared as nightmares throughout her sleep. Sara looked upon her with those soft brown eyes; she had a fine Indian-cocoa skin.

When she came back in to check the coffee, she found Owen sitting at the dining room table, with two cups served, and the cream and sugar on the table.

"Why didn't you tell me?" Owen said. "About Donny."

"Don't start this now. I'll answer anything you want to know, but not now. I can't talk about this anymore; I can't think about it either; and I can't *stop* thinking about it."

She had no real reason for letting him in. She did not know Owen, only that Paul had cared for him in a big way. She did not believe he had anything more to do with Paul's death than he had already told her. He had been in the wrong place at the wrong time. She knew that side of the coin. It had been that way with herself, right before the incident with Sara, and God knows, she could understand circumstance better than anyone alive.

She looked at his face as he sipped his coffee solemnly.

"Why the big greeting when I came in?" he asked her.

"I'm desperate. Can't you tell?"

"For what?"

"For somebody to touch my life with a magic wand and make this all a dream." The patch over his eye set his face out of balance. It made the long line of his nose look crooked, as if it had been broken. His good eye darted nervously around the table, as though it couldn't find a focus.

"Where's your sling?"

"I got rid of it. I don't need it anymore." He could not help feeling uneasy. Something was wrong. There was some kind of trick coming down on him. He could feel it. "Can you help me?" he asked.

"How?"

"I need money. Not from you. I want it from Donny and I'll need your car to get it."

"You're not leaving town?"

"I'm thinking about it."

"But what about helping me? What about getting that bastard to pay?"

"That's your problem."

"What about Paul? He was your friend. It's your problem too."

Owen saw him lying on the dock; he remembered how light he'd been as he dragged him through the water, and then how heavy he'd gotten when they'd carried him off the dock. Yes, that's my problem, he thought. One that I'll never unload.

"Come with me to the police," she said.

"Crosby went. That's enough. When they arrest Donny, I'll think about going to the police."

He drained his cup and poured another. "Could I have an egg or something?"

She pushed away from the table and went into the kitchen. From the refrigerator, she took a couple of eggs and cracked them into a pan of sizzling butter. She put bread in the toaster. "Where did you stay last night?" she asked again.

"Why are you trying to find out? What's with you? I'm not turning myself in, or letting myself get caught. Don't you understand?"

She reeled on him. Behind her, the burner was too hot and the black smoke of the burning butter rose above her. "You don't understand! You don't understand anything except saving your own ass." She ran from the kitchen.

She was becoming manic, he thought. One minute, she would be light and flitting about; the next, she would explode.

He took the burnt eggs off the range, popped the toast up and ate it dry. He watched her slip into *her* corner of the couch—the same way she had when he had come here the first time—and pull the blanket over her legs. She must have practiced that maneuver.

"I'm sorry about the eggs," she said when he came into the living room.

"I wasn't hungry anyway."

"I haven't slept. I haven't eaten. I've been taking pills and drinking this shit." She held up the glass, then, after a second, sipped from it. "I feel like I can't control anything. It's more than Paul to me, you know. Of course, you wouldn't know. I would have expected the cops to believe me. It's their business."

"Believing?"

"In a sense." She got up from the couch and fixed herself another drink at the vinyl-covered bar in the corner. Owen asked for a beer. He pulled out a joint and lit it. When she came back, he handed it to her.

"He smoked with you, didn't he? He never let me smoke, though he talked a lot about us getting high together. He said it reflected on his position at the university. I got to dislike him so terribly," she said. Her voice verged on tears. "It wasn't going anywhere."

"And Donny?" Owen said. He took the joint back from her and pulled the smoke deeply into his lungs. She went into a coughing fit from holding in the smoke so she chased it with a dollop of brandy.

"Can we stop this?" she said finally. "It makes me terribly depressed."

Owen did not know whether she meant the pot or the talk of Donny.

"Paul talked about you a lot," he said.

While she studied the contents of her glass, she said, "I suppose he would have had to. To someone." He sure as hell couldn't talk to me, she thought. He had told her once that he could never get over the feeling that everything he told her was a line that she must have heard in a club somewhere, and that was why he had difficulty expressing himself. It was like comparing dicks, he told her—although not in quite those words—and coming up short.

Owen asked if he could shower and shave. He wanted to clean himself up while he still had a chance. He did not know how long he'd have to stay on the river, and he thought a warm shower would be a small, pleasant memory to sustain him.

The bathroom was pink-tiled, with wicker shelves attached to the walls and hanging plants in baskets attached to the ceiling. There were dozens of shampoos, conditioners, rinses, combs and makeup jars scattered on the wicker shelving. The combined smell of all these things made the bathroom smell old, like they were accumulated over a long period of time by a person who had known, through vanity, what health brought.

In the shower, Owen struggled with strange feelings of déjà vu. It was as though he had been in this bathroom before, but he hadn't. As he soaped himself with the loofah sponge, he noticed he had an erection, and in that instant, he imagined Lorene in the shower with him. He would make her hold the towel rack above her head while he lathered the front of her body. It was a pleasant, sensual thought, and one of the few he had had since Sunday that didn't concern Paul's death. Then it hit him, like someone had turned off all the hot water and he was trapped against the cold tile by a spray of even colder water. These were the same type of sponges that hung from Donny's shower fixture. And the shampoos. In a claustrophobic panic, he whipped open the shower curtain, drenching the floor and rug with water. She had set up her own bathroom at Donny's.

He got out of the tub and toweled dry. He told himself: No, calm yourself. There is a rational explanation for all this. He wanted to tear the bottles from the shelves, and tear her, too, from where she sat on the couch.

A meal was waiting for him in the dining room. She had spread back the curtains and the early morning light arced across the big oak dining table to an antique, glass-front hutch in the corner, where china was placed in descending order of importance.

"I didn't have any bacon," she said. "I hope that's all right."

The place mat was set at the head of the table, with the utensils and napkins arranged precisely on the right-hand side. She had made him an omelet and potatoes, and poured him a small glass of juice and a large cup of coffee. She was too much of a contradiction, he thought, as he tried controlling the new rage that threatened to erupt from his abdomen.

"Thank you," he said, and fell somberly to eating.

She noticed that something in his attitude had changed since he had come from the shower. His eye had a madly intense focus to it now. It searched the plate before him like a spotlight, but he would not lift his head. She had wanted a smile—something human, sensitive—from somebody. Even if he had had something to do with Paul's death. That's all it would take, she thought, to make me feel like a person now.

Her robe folded open below her neck, revealing the inverted crescents of her full, unsupported breasts. An oily sheen made her skin glow in the morning light, and it fueled his rage even more. How could she sit there, so gentle, so fragile, with an aura of light emanating from her, with those slack green eyes so clear that he could see the miniature outline of his hunched form at the table, with those lips so thick and full . . . How could she be mixed up in anything with that sonofabitch.

"I'm becoming unglued." Her voice trembled slightly.

"We all are," Owen said abruptly.

"But it's worse for me. Death makes you think about things most people never have the sensitivity to think about

168

otherwise. But I think about those things all the time. Yes," she said, "it's worse for me."

"Bullshit. There's no quality to badness. Bad is bad. The difference comes in the way you handle things."

"I was crazy once."

"We're all crazy," Owen said. "All the time."

"I can't talk to you," she snapped, slamming her open palm on the table. "Can't you see how much I need this? And every time I say something, you pop off some bullshit judgment."

He was confused. Instantly, she had made him feel like he was the one who was crazy, that he had no right even to think the thoughts about her and Donny. And that his self-fulfilling rage—he knew that's what it was—would find no vent against her.

"I'm sorry," he said, but she had already left the table and was taking a pill from the vial on the coffee table.

He pushed aside his plate. "Hey, don't do that," he said. She swallowed it. "What kind of pill was that?"

"Valium." She washed it down with some brandy. "I eat these like you smoke pot," she said, falling back into the couch. He stood for a moment, staring at the gray abstract of the listing ship, or the wolf. It seemed to change every time he looked at it, like one of those 3-D Crackerjacks rings.

"It's not just Paul," she said. "Though that's enough. This has happened before in my life. Or something like this. With a girl named Sara Halfacre."

"The same thing that happened to Paul, happened to your friend?"

"Not exactly. No," she said, "the same thing never happens twice, but it was close enough. Things like this ought not happen to someone more than once. Why don't you light another one of those joints. I'm feeling better now."

She looked like she was in control again. The lines of her

brow faded, became softer, and Owen tried imagining the complex chemistry that was working inside her. The pills, the brandy and whiskey, and now the pot. It seemed to bring her up, then smash her down. But she was up now, and she was glowing.

He took another joint from his shirt pocket and lit it. "You shouldn't mix all this shit," he said, but he didn't believe it. She looked like she could use it. Her brown robe, slightly opened, showed the roundness of one of her breasts. He followed a line of tendon up her neck to the sharp line·of her jaw. He ached for her intensely.

"What happened with Sara?" he asked as he took the joint back.

"You know how I got the name Lorene? It means 'light of life.' My momma gave it to me. She used to say that I was the light of her life. Said I brought her and Daddy luck." Her eyes drifted from his face to some point behind him.

She was dangerous, he thought. That was the feeling that he had gotten when she opened the front door for him. There was something wrong with the way she was acting. It could have been the pills. There was more than just Valium in that vial. And feeling what she was feeling, while mixing what she was mixing, made him scared that she'd flip.

"Daddy was a coalminer. Deeply religious. He used to say that light of life stuff was hogwash. The money he got— and he got a lot—the day I was born was the result of God's will and a good insurance man. He used to say, 'That child's no sign at all.' But Momma told me I was, just the same. She put my first bra on me when I was ten years old. She told me I'd be nothing but a good sign for whoever got me; but it didn't work out that way at all."

The pot was working on Owen now, and he tried imagining Lorene at ten. He saw her father with the permanent black stain from the coal about his face and eyes.

He saw him stooped and lanky and full of hellfire and brimstone. He saw that tender scene too, with Lorene and her mother as she fastened the straps behind her, carefully cupping and adjusting her daughter's new breasts in the wire-hard bra. Her hair must have been red like Lorene's, only softer, fuller, longer. He thought, too, that there would be another Plymouth outside the house soon, if it weren't there already, and his little fantasy burst inside him like a balloon full of water.

"Sara was a friend of mine when I was twelve. God, what a beautiful girl she was. She had cocoa-brown skin and straight dark hair and eyes like little black buttons. I always wished I'd grow up as beautiful as her, but then she didn't grow up at all. The town I grew up in had a sickness."

"A sickness?" Owen said.

"Not the kind you'd think of at first. Not a medical sickness, but there was something strange. It began in the middle of that year. There was a paranoia that reached epidemic proportions."

"How can a whole town be paranoid?" Owen sat up on the rug and held her eyes steadily. The feeling of danger was coming back now. He was trapped between a rock and a hard place, he thought, with her spacing out on some childhood horror story while the house was being staked out outside. He had promised himself in the woods last night that he would be more careful.

"Nobody on the streets would talk to each other. Not hello. Not the time of day. Nothing," she said. "And I'm not making that up. We were right across the state line from Garden City, Kansas, where that family had been brutally murdered. They made a movie about it. I didn't know what it was then, but now I think everybody suspected everybody else. Our town was half-Indian and half-white and each group believed the other to be the devil incarnate. Men carried guns on the street and Daddy said he'd blow the brains out of the first one that stepped near his family—Indian or white. Said it was the will of God. He was big on the will of God."

The first thought that came to Owen as he lay back on the rug was: This is too much. But he knew that it was not too much. No more than anything else. Death turned people into all manner of unrecognizable forms. It took shape in the pink, limp and lifeless body of his teacher, and the mantra of that lunatic Donny—I am not a bad man—and in the shape too of this woman who sat with him in the semi-darkness telling of a sickness from the past with vacant eyes while her tit slipped out of her open robe. No, this was not too much.

She had given Sara the name Fauna as they played in the woods one day. They had met each other there. Sara had snuck away from the reservation, and Lorene from her house. They did it often in that twelfth year. They hid in the trees from each other and played games of tracking and hunting. Sometimes they imagined themselves deer and ran full tilt through the sparse woods. Sara always ran first and fastest, her long hair whipping her brown bony shoulders. When they finally collapsed from exhaustion, sweat matting the hair to their foreheads and cheeks, they would lie in the pine straw and look at each other.

"I loved her," Lorene said. "She was what I wished I could have been. The men watched me on the streets all the time, and I used to hear them make remarks about my body. I ignored them. I was too scared to do anything else, and when Sara and I used to lie there in the grass, sweating and breathing like we'd just escaped the hunter, I'd say little things to myself. 'Why couldn't I look like her?' Everyone left her alone."

And in that year, Sara's half-brother had taken too much whiskey and found Lorene coming home from the woods. She got in his pickup quite naturally, expecting a ride home, but he had driven her out past where she lived, past even the reservation, and she began to panic. He put one of his thick tawny hands on her breast as he drove and the truck swerved. She said, "Please, David, stop it." But he was too intense in some drunken chanting he had been doing, and he pinched her breasts hard.

The bangs of his black hair shaped his overlarge face and dipped to a point above his nose. He had a small protruding brow that cast full shadows over his small watering eyes. His massive jaw hung heavy like a cow's, and he carried her easily out of the cab and threw her in the flatbed. He did not rip her clothes; he carefully removed her blouse and bra, then her shorts. He rolled her over, and with her face pushed into a broken bale of hay, he took her from behind.

"I blamed it on Sara, though I knew it wasn't her fault. Every time I saw her face after that, I thought of that big drooling bastard and I got so frightened I couldn't talk. He told me afterwards that if I opened my mouth, he'd peel my hair off my head with the bowie knife he wore on his belt. He said it would go worse on me than that family in Garden City. I told Sara I hated her and never saw her again."

For two years it continued. Whenever Sara's brother found her alone, he'd carry her off. The men in town had gotten more abrasive in their remarks to her on the street, as if the word were getting around. And once toward the end, she had enjoyed it. Not the rape itself, nor the sour smell of the hunched man behind her—he could never do it looking at her face—what she had enjoyed was the intense liquid feeling deep in the center of her belly.

When she was fourteen, Sara disappeared. Someone had seen a pickup pull over, and saw her hop in. At first, they said it looked like David's truck so they didn't think anything about it. But then they said there seemed to be something funny about the *way* her feet left the ground; they seemed like they had been jerked. Lorene thought, too, that it had been David and that the sickness was spreading.

"I felt sorry for her. I knew exactly what they were doing to her. But I remember feeling glad too, in a way. I would be able to be her friend again. I could look in her face and not see David."

The sheriff didn't find her for a week, and when he did, he found her tied to a tree. She had been bludgeoned repeatedly and the brick, with pieces of scalp and hair stuck to it, lay beside her on the ground.

"I snapped. I had to go into analysis after that. Can you imagine that? Being a fourteen-year-old on a shrink's couch? There was a whole long time, maybe a month, when I didn't say a single word to anyone except, 'There ain't no light to life.' And I believed it with all my heart when my daddy said I wasn't no sign at all."

"And now it's happened again," Owen said sullenly. He watched her eyes. They betrayed nothing of what she was feeling, nothing of what she had just told him. They held a glazed, empty, doped look.

She sat up and adjusted the robe. "I'm coming all apart." She cinched the belt tighter and smoothed the lace collar.

But what about now, Owen thought. What about Donny and Paul? Where do these pieces fit?

"I took the name Fauna because I have this crazy thing in me. I hate to think of Sara, and I can only think that it should have been me. I think of the last thing I told her —how I hated her—and all this comes to me in an instant every time I see my name on a marquee."

"Everybody has that, I think," he said. The sour smell that filled the room where Paul's clothes lay heaped instantly filled his nose.

"But not like me. I was screwed around so much that I didn't know which way was up half the time. I only remem-

174

ber the horrifying things *he* used to tell me about what he'd do to my family—and the once it felt good, in that single instance, I liked him."

Owen looked at her strangely. He got up to see if the Plymouth was outside again. The whole time she had been telling him the story, the thought of the car sitting in the street held his attention. It was like walking with a pebble in his shoe.

"You think that's strange," she said, watching him part the curtains.

"Strange that you got off on Sara's brother?" He looked back at her. She was sitting up straight on the couch with the glass to her lips and the golden liquor draining into her mouth. "Only moderately so. The cops aren't back."

"It was like that with my dancing too. I hated those leches out there because they all looked at me like David. But I loved them too. I knew they couldn't have me, but I knew how much they wanted me. I could feel that agony in them and I got off on it."

"Is that the way you felt about Paul?"

Lorene looked as though she had seen Sara's ghost. Her face—the smooth, radiant skin—slackened and she hissed, "You sonofabitch."

She sprung from the couch and disappeared down the hall. He knew it was stupid to have said that now, and he wished that he could call the words back. He heard sobbing coming from the back of the house, deep convulsive sobs punctuated by high-pitched talking. But he had to know. He had to tie these things together in his head. Crosby had opened a whole can of worms inside him, telling him about this affair she had had with Donny. She had not grieved the way she should have when he was first with her, and those two things—the affair and the strange way she handled Paul's death—tossed him in and out of an uncontrolled anger. He looked at the picture again, the rage of the wolf, the storm and the ship. He wanted to remove it from the wall and place it face down on the rug.

Standing at the door to her room, he said, "You never answered my question."

"Go away," she said. She was lying on the bed. "You go away and I'll go away, and we'll both have nightmares the rest of our lives. Paul can be dead and Donny can go on to become governor or whatever he wants to be and the rest of the world can go suck air."

"I have to know that answer. I have to believe it." She squirmed under his pressure. "Did you love him or hate him?" He had to hear the words, to check them against what he thought was right, ultimately to check them against what he knew sanity to be now.

"Both," she said into the pillow. Her hair had come loose, and against the flowered pattern on the pillow case, it fanned out symmetrically like a delicate oriental fan.

"You can't have both," he said.

"I can." She whirled from the pillow; her eyes were puffed red, her nostrils flared. The robe fell open around her breasts. "I can have it any way I want. It was going to end between Paul and me. But not so I could take up with Donny. That was a dead-end street. Donny knew me from a long time ago; that was my tie to him. I was going to leave this summer, after Paul got through with school, so it wouldn't mess him up in the middle of a quarter. So it wouldn't ruin his job."

Owen watched her breasts heave as she talked. They were marvelously heavy and her nipples stood out hard and brown against the pearlescent whiteness.

"No," Lorene said. "I didn't love him and I didn't hate him. I had gotten to feel toward him like I did toward the men who watched me in the clubs. I thought being a house-wife would save me, but I was wrong." She caught Owen

176

looking at her breasts and she pulled the robe around her. "Now, get out," she said, lying back into the pillow.

Owen sat in the rocking chair beside the bed. "I didn't want it to be this way," he said.

She would not look at him. She searched for patterns among the speckled chips of stucco on her white ceiling.

Owen looked around the room. It was distinctly hers. There was lace everywhere. Around the skirt on the vanity full of makeup and cold creams, around the bedspread and pillows. Around her robe too. Delicate, frilly white lace as fine as the pale smooth skin of her breasts. He wanted to scream: *Let me have you!* Any way at all.

A picture on her chest of drawers was toppled over a jewelry box. It looked like it had been thrown. He righted it. A splinter of glass was lying on top of the chest and a corner of the cheap gold frame was bent. It was a picture of her in full costume—all spangles, rhinestones and ostrich feathers.

Her hands were jauntily posed on her hips. The rhinestone choker around her neck insinuated itself down through her cleavage. Large rhinestone fingers cupped her naked breasts and larger rhinestones dangled below them. The G-string she wore was white silk with an intricate sequined paisley design set square in the center of her sex. Her legs straddled some imaginary horse and were covered with white ostrich-feather chaps that flared at the bottom. Scrawled in almost indecipherable blue ink in the corner was the inscription: To Donny, Remember me this way. Love Fauna.

A burning sensation climbed from deep in his belly. It was the feeling he had had when he stood over Donny's sink, retching his guts out. He had handled his misunderstanding well up till now, he thought. Since sometime Sunday, he had managed to place each little piece of this horror in some rational perspective and he was finding that he could accept

177

almost anything. But now he turned on her. "What kind of shit have you been handing me?"

"I don't know what you're talking about." Her voice equaled his in indignation.

"This picture." He gripped the picture in both hands.

She rolled from the bed, agile as a cat, and snatched it from him. "I went to his house when he wasn't there and took it. Besides, it's none of your business," she said. "That's past. That's over."

"I don't believe you. You probably cooked this whole thing up with Donny, you fucking whore. You're not going to hang this . . ."

She screamed as she struck him on the face and he fell back a step. Before the sting had begun to burn his cheek, he had his hand raised and brought it down across her shoulder. His balance changed with the quick movement and he did not know if it was because he had hit her once already or if it was the release from the horror of the last two days, but his hand was already on its way again before he tried to stop it.

Lorene flew backwards against the bed. "I hate you," she screamed.

He was on top of her, straddling her shoulders with his knees. He had caught the hysteria which she had contained so well and he looked down on her from some manic height. His hands froze in front of his chest; his fingers curled in like claws. A jolting energy coursed through each cell of his body, pounding behind his eyes. He had flashes of the sponges in both Donny's and her showers. The sickening foul smell of rubber hung in his nose. In a moment, he saw her too. Donny was dusting her off, just as he had dusted Paul off before dropping him over the edge. At this moment, he thought, she was the weaker one, the one he was going to dump on.

178

She kept twisting her head from side to side. "Let me alone, you sonofabitch," she cried. "Let me up."

He clamped her head and kissed her lips as hard as he had hit her. Her robe had come open and he could feel the heat of her chest through his jeans, on the underside of his legs.

He slid down the length of her body, working his knees between her shut thighs, spreading them, still pinning her arms. Beads of sweat glistened on her forehead. He took her full nipple into his mouth and she stopped fighting. A light salt taste worked on the roof of his mouth and he closed his eyes.

"You bastard," she growled.

When he looked up, it was Sara's face he saw. Just as Lorene described it to him—though now there was madness fueling the sharp-boned chocolate features. Slowly, he released his grip.

He knelt up between her legs. Her arms fell limp beside her head. She was breathing heavily through her mouth. The green of her eyes crackled like hot sparks. He knew that if he touched her bare skin, some whirling inferno would rise up and consume him. He pulled her robe closed and left the room without a word.

CHAPTER

OWEN LEFT LORENE'S BY THE BACK DOOR WITHOUT CHECKING the front. If that white Plymouth outside earlier had been his own paranoia, so much the better. He wouldn't be any less careful. And if they weren't watching for him now, they would be soon enough.

He decided to take lunch at a health food restaurant across from the university, then figure out some discreet way to contact Donny for the money. After that, he would drive out to the river and bide his time till he could make a safe escape.

He bought the afternoon edition of the *Putnam Daily* outside and climbed the steep, garishly painted stairs to the restaurant.

A short man with an unnaturally soft voice and long curly hair asked him if he'd prefer a table to the counter, and seated him in a corner by the window. He was surrounded by huge plants, leaning toward him at all manner of angles. A light vegetable oil aroma mixed with the smell of fresh black soil, and filled his corner. The faint insistent tinsel sound of sitar music wafted to him from strategically placed speakers.

"Hello," his waitress said. "Would you like to see a menu?" Her hair was pulled back and tied behind her head. She had a slight overbite and wore an obscenely beautiful smile. The outline of her breasts showed through her loose gauze blouse.

"Yes," he said. "And a glass of water with no ice."

"You got it." She turned and whisked away.

He flopped open the paper and saw Donny's picture on the front page. "Local Lawyer Leads House Race." With thirty percent of the vote counted, the paper predicted Donny's victory. The picture looked like it had been taken at a portrait studio for his high school graduation. His hair looked wet and plastered to his head. The line of his smile was embarrassingly crooked; and without shadows, his close-set eyes gave the appearance of being crossed.

"You ready to order?" the waitress asked. Her voice slid into his distraction like part of the music.

"Vegetarian crepe with a glass of Heineken. No chopsticks."

"Care for rolls?"

"Nothing more."

She gave him a puzzled look before she left. He wondered if he had said something funny. Or if he had something—a piece of food—stuck in his teeth.

He did not read the paper while he ate. He tried to focus all his concentration in his mouth. It was the only thing he could do that had no connection to Sunday. It seemed as though everything that had happened in his life before, and everything that had happened since, funneled through this one point in time. It could go on like that forever unless he could step in and change it. Eat, he told himself. The crepe was light, stuffed with a smooth combination of broccoli, carrots and sauce. His waitress appeared again at his side, and while his mouth was full, asked, "Is everything all right? Do you like it?"

He nodded his head.

He saved the whole glass of beer for the end, then downed it in a single effort. He signaled for another one.

She wore cloth slippers under her long flowered skirt. That accounted for her ability to sneak up on you, he thought. When she brought the beer back, she hovered around the table. He was about to ask her if there was something the matter when he realized she was looking at his patch. The adhesive at the top had come loose and he reached up and pressed it to his forehead. She flashed her sharp white teeth and turned away.

He sipped the second beer slowly and went through the paper. He knew he would have to devise some plan to get the money from Donny, but he wanted a little while where he wouldn't have to think about that—a short break from it all. He was no longer high and he cursed himself for not taking one of Lorene's pills when he left. Though she needed them—all of them—a hell of a lot worse than I, he thought.

In the back of the second section of the paper, a small article caught his eyes. "City Elder Found Dead." It began, in bold print:

Arnold R. Crosby, 83, a Putnam Hall resident for nearly fifty years, was found dead in his sleep early this morning. A concerned neighbor checked on him when he failed to answer the phone. Putnam Hall's medical examiner, Dr. Richard Wesley, attributed the cause of death to heart failure. Crosby, who had founded Construction Equipment, Inc., retired to Putnam Hall at the age of thirty-five after selling his business to a consortium of south Florida construction companies. He maintained a small farm just outside the town limits and took an active hand in shaping the growth and politics of the area. Crosby is survived . . .

Owen stared at Crosby's name in print. There had to be some kind of mistake. He had been with Crosby only yesterday afternoon. They had eaten fish together. They had . . . There was no mistake though. Newspapers don't print these kinds of things unless they're true. A rush of panic coursed through him; his fingers tweaked spasmodically, making the paper dance. Something between a scream and tears backed up in his throat. The sunshine on the waitress's face was replaced with worry; her brow knitted. She said, "You feel all right? Is there something I can do?"

Her voice had lowered an octave as though she were speaking for the concern of all mankind, for all the enlightened ones. In that moment he hated the sound of her voice more than he hated anything. She did not merit that type of complacency. For true peace of mind, you had to go through trials. Crosby had impressed that upon him. Setbacks, he said, give you the opportunity to test the resources of your spirit.

Owen wanted to get up and leave, but he didn't have anywhere to go. His past was so diffused now, that all he had was the present. And that was too bleak to think about. He wanted someone to go to, to cry to, to scream the primal scream of life to. He thought that, at any second, his insides were going to blow out all over the restaurant. His entrails would be scattered over the finely manicured plants, and on the people who sat among them. The music pitched back and forth between subdued chimes and the frantic fingerwork of some imagined players. Owen had visions of the kitchen help sitting with their legs folded underneath them and facing east in some prayerful meditation. He put enough money on the table to cover his bill and ran out.

He walked past Paul's office but couldn't summon the strength to go in. He could not see that melancholy bust of Tennyson with the cowboy hat. These were the incongruities that drove you unexplainably to strange things, he thought. Yes, and the election results and the death notice in the same paper, separated by all the news that's fit to print.

He was taken with a great urge to lift right off the planet, to fly. He would head straight for the sun and slowly, with each beat of his long powerful wings, he would ascend and burn away the gnawing intensity of his new life, his changed life, until he got close enough to be consumed by the flames themselves. Somehow death would draw him gloriously upward above the thermals that bathed the earth, into the vortex of all life.

□ □

When he knocked on Lorene's back door, it was nearly five o'clock. He had smoked a joint and drunk some wine. He had eaten and he had cried, and he said to her, "I didn't have anywhere to go."

"Come in," she said.

"No. Come out."

She cocked her head and looked at him strangely. "Let me change."

"Bring Paul's binoculars," he called behind her.

He could not go inside. He needed to stay on the porch to maintain a communion with the air. His grief rippled off him in waves, like heat from a highway. Being closed in would only serve to boil what was going on inside him.

Lorene wore her hair in a pony tail. Her jeans were rolled to the calf and her wooden clogs made loud clacking sounds as she walked out of the house and onto the porch. She looked younger to Owen, like a student from the university. She had more faces than a siren, he thought.

"Meet me at the end of the alley. In the shopping center parking lot."

When she picked him up, he said, "Do you know how to get to Newnan's Lake?"

"You'll have to direct me."

He spoke only to give her the necessary directions. Once though, he had excitedly pointed out a large red-shouldered hawk to her as it streaked from the roadside underbrush to the top of some telephone wires. "Looks like a fat old man," she had said, "with a big pot belly."

She stole glances at his profile as she drove. The adhesive of his eye patch was beginning to curl and blacken with dirt. His cheeks looked clawed with fatigue and he slumped in the seat with his foot propped on the dashboard. It occurred to her then that he needed her as much, or maybe more, than she needed him.

"You want me to stop?" she asked. "Get some more stuff for your eye?"

"No."

Lorene turned off the road at Owen's instructions and they bounced into the irregularly filled concrete parking lot of McElvay's fish camp.

"Park over there." He pointed to a live oak, under which sat a line of cars and pickups, all with empty trailers.

It was a perfect day for spotting eagles. Warm and bright, with a stiff breeze coming in off the lake. Ripples of heat undulated above the surface. The lake was so big that he couldn't make out the boats on the far bank, fishing under the cypress stands, with his naked eye.

Lorene followed him down a cement landing to the water's edge. Small black minnows dotted the shallows and bobbed in the lapping brown water.

She wore some strange sweet perfume that came from behind him and like a gauze cloud wrapped his head with a magnolia scent. He saw an osprey first, low and circling. Where there's ospreys, there's eagles, he said to himself.

Crosby's rule. Then a shadow hovered above the osprey, darkening it, and he didn't have to raise the glasses to know it was up there. His heart clicked and he felt immediately better. He not only *wanted* to see an eagle today, he *needed* to see one. Just as on the Ocklawaha, with the Group, when the eagle had circled them, something inside him grew high and light and he became the eagle. He was soaring.

He handed the glasses to Lorene. "Look," he said, pointing high into the white sky at the straight-winged silhouette. "There's what started this whole mess."

At first she had trouble adjusting the binoculars; then she drew the bird into focus. "That's an eagle?" She held the glasses out in front of her and looked at them as if something were wrong with them. "I've never seen one before."

"Consider yourself lucky."

"It wasn't worth it all," she said, pressing the glasses tight to her eyes. Her head was craned back and her larynx made an unseemly knot in the smooth twine of her neck muscles.

"Crosby's dead too," he said. He didn't know what else to say. The words surfaced through the thickness of his tongue on their own and formed themselves into words.

She dropped the glasses on the cement slab and Owen caught them as they slid toward the tannic-stained water. "No!"

An aluminum boat sputtered to the landing in front of them. Two small men dressed in bulky army surplus camouflage waved to them. The man in the bow threw Owen his line and he pulled them in. The man in the stern shot a stream of tobacco juice into the water and thanked him.

"Come on," he said to Lorene. He wondered why people's first reaction to death was always an emphatic No, as if there were some way, by denying it, they could make it all a lie.

He stopped in front of a neat row of upturned olive-colored skiffs by the water's edge. Off to the side, on the dock, a teenager struggled to tie up his boat by the gas pump. The two men in camouflage were off-loading their equipment and goodnaturedly trading licks in the arm. They popped open beer cans and sprayed foam at each other.

"It was in the same paper as Donny's election results." He scanned the sky for the eagle again, but he could not find it. He focused on a bald spot across the lake and worked slowly, patiently upward.

"How?" she asked.

"Paper said heart failure."

"Do you believe it?"

"Why not?" he said. "It had to happen sooner or later. He was old." There's no such thing as believing, Owen told himself, not anymore. "Goddamnit, where's that eagle?" He finally dropped the glasses to his side.

The wind off the lake was whipping the ends of Lorene's pony tail. She had an intensely sad look on her face and two lines, lightened with makeup, spread from the corners of her eyes.

"But he wasn't weak." Her eyes fluttered, then half closed. "He wasn't sick."

"Let's walk out to the point. Maybe we'll see the nest from there." He knew what she was getting at. It had been beating around inside him since the restaurant, but all he could think of now was, Find the eagle again.

A couple of older bass fishermen sat with cans of beer on the dock, talking and looking down into their boat reverently. As Owen and Lorene passed, one of them made a remark and Lorene called them pigs.

McElvay had constructed the point out of fill to serve as a cove to protect the sailboats moored inside. On rough days, the wind howled over the lake and buffeted even the most securely tied boats. The point had grown weedy, except for a trail that led out to a clearing at its tip.

"Those are kites," Owen said. Small white birds darted low above the water in front of them. One after another, the kites pulled their wings into their sides and plummeted twenty feet to the water, disappearing in a translucent roil of bubbles. Then they would surface and fly away with silver specks of minnows in their beaks.

"There it is," Owen said, "above that stand of cypress." He glassed the trees from the point and saw the nest on one of the lower branches, shielded from above by larger, overhanging ones. "It's circling the nest."

He handed Lorene the binoculars and sat at her feet in the clearing. The water lapped at the packed rocks and fill of the point. She stood with her feet together as if she had been called to attention. He looked at the V of her well-defined calf muscles. There was no sign of stubble on her legs and the skin around her heels was dry and cracking.

"Is that the same one?" The small of her back arched nicely, and with her elbows high and her shirt puffed out by the wind, she looked mannish.

"Could be. I can't tell that well. Crosby could tell. He knew everything about eagles."

"Is he protecting the nest? Is that why he's flying like that?"

"I can't say. He could be just soaring. Playing. Anything. I don't know what he's doing. Nobody ever knows what an eagle is doing. Mostly, they just guess."

She sat beside him, wiping her hands and brushing back loose strands of hair. The bird was dark against an absolute blue brightness of sky and there was an angle to its circle where they could see its white head and tail glint so sharply in the sun that it looked like a flash of fire.

"You want to hear something neat?"

"Pleeease," Lorene exaggerated. The sheer desperation made Owen laugh. Then Lorene caught the hysteria and they were both howling into the wind.

Wiping tears from his eye, Owen said, "What's neat is the courting ritual of these birds."

"Neat?" she said and gave a small laugh.

"A holdover from the last decade. Anyway, the male flies above the female, calling to her and she turns on her back as she's flying and extends her talons upward to him. Then he takes them, and they both fold their wings back over their heads, like this." He extended his arms behind him at 45° angles. "Then they cartwheel to the ground, singing back and forth all the time." His hands tumbled in front of his face and Lorene watched them intently. "Just before they hit the ground, after falling two or three hundred feet, they break apart and zoom straight to their highest height." His hands fell to the dirt beside him.

"Beats hell out of the way people do it," she said, and again they broke into manic sobs of laughter.

Lorene noticed that when he talked, his hands shook. She reached into her shirt pocket and pulled out a tissue. Unwrapping it, she said, "You want one of these?"

"Where'd you get Seconal?"

"I just got them," she said. "You want one?"

He thought it would be a mistake but he took one anyway and swallowed it.

"May I look some more?" she said, taking the glasses from Owen and standing up.

"I'm sorry about getting so carried away."

"Did the Group ever come here?"

"Sure. It was Crosby who showed us all that nest." He pointed in the direction she was looking.

She watched the eagle for a while longer. Several vultures now soared with the eagle, taunting it, but each time the eagle changed its circle to their direction, they scattered.

"Donny had something to do with it, you know. I believe that. I believe he had something to do with Crosby's death." She talked fast now and turned to look down on him where he sat.

"You're as crazy as I am."

189

"Crazier. I was almost ready to cave in." She balled her fists and put them on her hips. The upcurve of her eyeliner and the half-shadow cutting her face gave her a devilish appearance.

"We can do something about him," he said.

"You'll go to the police with me?"

"Not on your life."

She knelt down in front of him and hugged him around the shoulders. She could feel an imperceptible tremble, like the hum of an engine about to go awry, move over the muscles of his shoulder blades and into his spine.

"No," she said. "No police."

□ □

Georgia set up a small portable television on an end table she had dragged into the conference room of Donny's office so he could watch the returns come in. She had fixed him an egg salad sandwich and it sat untouched on the floor beside him. From behind, he looked to her like an old man sunk deeply into the green vinyl chair. The hair at the back of his neck was jagged around the collar of his wrinkled denim shirt.

"Eat something, will ya," she said. "You're a winner."

Because she had slept through the night, she hadn't called her husband. When she woke up, near dawn, Donny was in bed beside her, awake. She remembered thinking that they fit nicely together. He rounded into the curve of her back and buttocks like spoons in a matched set.

She called her husband from the office right after they opened up. She had told him that they'd fallen asleep in the conference room, exhausted from the final duties of the campaign. Working on speeches. Acceptance speeches. Speeches in case there was a runoff. And, of course, one should he lose. She could see Chuck's gaunt, ragged face on the other end of the line. The gold-capped center tooth and the grease, the perpetual grease of his life and hers, under his fingernails. "You're a whore and a liar," he shouted at her. She hung up on him.

Now there was something wrong with Donny. He made her feel like she had been used. Like she felt after going down on that boy in high school. She wanted to ask him: Didn't I do good for you? Didn't I satisfy you?

He wouldn't touch the sandwich and he hadn't so much as kissed her or come up from behind her like he loved to do, to squeeze her tits. He just sat there with the lights dimmed, staring at the gray glow from the television set with the sound turned so low you couldn't hear it.

"Want me to get us a bottle of champagne to celebrate?"

"Yeah," he said. "And bring me a pack of cigarettes. The brand you smoke."

When he heard the latch on the front door click, he ambled down the corridor to his office and drew open the drapes. His office faced south and the afternoon sunlight bent around the corner of the building and splashed yellow over the mess of work on his desk. He fixed himself a Scotch and water and finished it in three healthy swallows.

From the closet in the corner, he took his briefcase and opened it on his desk. There was a client file in it that he had thought he lost. Finding it gave him a moment of satisfaction, like finding a missing piece of himself, though the case had long since resolved itself.

He emptied the contents of the briefcase—a few pens, legal pads, a text on successful cross-examination strategy—onto his desk and took Crosby's revolver from the drawer.

The sheer weight of it frightened him. He popped open the cylinder and each chamber contained a bullet. He slid one bullet out, lined up the empty chamber with the hammer, and clicked it closed. The gun's blue steel finish was covered with a film of light oil and he held it close to his nose. It brought back the night, as he had sat in Crosby's chair with the barrel of the .38 pressed to his lips. The cold of the steel, the imagined impact as the bullet slammed through his pitifully thin skull, the taste—that salt taste of sulfur on his tongue. He had carried that taste with him the whole way back to the cabin. Back to Georgia curled into a tangle of covers. It would have been so easy just then. One spasm, one twitch of the finger.

The persistent tapping of someone's ring on the glass of the front door startled him. Deliberately, he did not answer. Instead, he put the gun in his briefcase and clamped it shut.

"One more drink," he said aloud. "And maybe a little sleep."

He had not slept after he left Crosby's. He doubted that he would ever sleep again. Each time he closed his eyes, he saw Crosby's face, stretched in some fabulous insuck of breath that would not come. His hands still carried the touch of Crosby's chest, the plastic feel of cold skin. Trying to save him was the worst thing he could have done. He should have just bolted from the house when he heard that feeble old fuck shuffling after the gun. By kneading his chest and trying to pound the life back into it, he had tainted the deepest recesses of his psyche. With Paul it had been different. It had been so much an accident, so much nobody else could ever know. He could not feel the pull of Paul's body through the water, and it would not have served anyone then to see justice done. Not at the expense of his life. But with Crosby, he had felt the exact moment his life passed out, felt it in his hands and on the inside of his thighs as he straddled the old man's hips. It was as though the old man had completely deflated in a single instant.

A shadow passed over his desk and he looked up to see Georgia at the plate glass window. She must have hopped the picket fence that surrounded the patio. He pushed himself out of the chair and opened the door.

"Didn't you hear me at the front door?"

"I'm sorry. No," he said.

"I forgot my keys." She threw him the pack of Winstons. "I forgot but you can't buy booze on election day in this county. You shoulda known that, Counselor."

"Slipped my mind. Want a drink of hard liquor?"

"Lot of stuff's slipping your mind." She sauntered to the desk and lay back over the mess, back over the briefcase too, and hiked her shirt. "Fix me a whiskey and come over here and get you some." She was mimicking the drawl of the Barkum woman who Donny had just gotten off. It was a little joke they shared when the tension ran high in the campaign. She licked her finger and traced wet concentric circles over her small hard breasts, each closing on the next till she took the nipple, which stood like a Hershey's kiss, between her fingers and rolled it.

"Pull your shirt down," Donny said. He filled a tumbler with whiskey and brought it to her. "And get off the desk."

"I'm gonna slap your face," she said. Her own face flushed scarlet as she tucked in her shirt. "I'm gonna get a decent job if you don't start treating me better." She was pouting now, playing some game she no doubt played with her hick husband, Donny thought.

"I need you to do something important for me," he told her. "So don't be a smartass." He called her that affectionately, when she started acting like a rowdy adolescent. "I need you to help me without asking any questions."

"Right, boss." She straightened immediately, picked up the legal pad he had removed from his briefcase, and one of the pens. "I'm ready."

"Stop fooling around, goddamnit, and put the pad down. I want you to take my passbook and go to the bank and draw out five thousand dollars."

"Fi . . ."

He cut her off. "Don't ask any questions."

She shifted impatiently from foot to foot. She was dying from frustration. It showed in the lines of her face, in the way she unwittingly pulled her eyebrows together over her black eyes. Her lips mouthed the words: Five thousand dollars.

The phone rang on Georgia's desk and she spun around and ran through the door. He could hear her muffled voice. She was putting off whoever was calling. He pressed the intercom. "It's all right, Georgia. I'll take the call."

"He was so persistent," she said back into the intercom. Her voice had a tinny distortion to it.

"You did right," he said. "Now go to the bank."

Again he waited till he heard the latch click on the front door; then he pressed the lighted button on his phone.

"Donny Waldo speaking," he said.

The other end was dead. He repeated himself.

"I'm gonna make this short," Owen said. "I want the money and I want it by tomorrow. Maybe the cops don't know and maybe they do, but I know and Lorene knows that you had something to do with Crosby's dying."

"Get fucked!" Donny screamed.

"You're the only one who's going to get fucked. I want out. Fauna," he exaggerated her name for Donny's sake, "Fauna wants out too."

"Are you *sure* there's a way out?"

"I know where you put Paul," Owen said. "I can do you in. You forced me to come with you, remember." Donny couldn't believe that Owen was sneering at him.

He sat on top of his desk and tore open the pack of cigarettes Georgia had gotten him. He fumbled with the match before he lit one. This was just what he needed, he thought, to snap him out of his apocalyptic depression. The surrogate son and recent widow tapping his well for goodies. Why had he been so worried?

"Where do I meet you?" he asked, flicking an ash on his rug.

"On the Ocklawaha. The place where we camped with the Group."

"You could hardly expect me to remember that place. It was nearly a year ago and that was the only time I'd ever gone there. Could you make it a bit simpler for me?"

"I'll tie up a marker so you'll know."

"This is funny," Donny said.

"It's not funny." There was an interminable silence on the line. "It's sick," Owen said finally.

CHAPTER

10

OWEN HUNG HIS ARM OUT THE WINDOW AS LORENE DROVE. The wind tore at it as if it weren't part of his body; his hair whipped around and stung his cheek. The Seconal he took seduced him away from the perilous chasm he had courted all day and settled him complacently now in the passenger seat of her car. His muscles were so limp from the drug that he felt as if he had just come from the table of a heavy-handed masseur.

With great effort, he said, "We can't go back to your place." His mouth was dry. "We'll get the boat and wait on the river."

Lorene nodded her head in agreement. Her eyes held the road with some violent determination. The line of her nose was straight; its tip turned up at an imperceptible angle.

He wondered if it hadn't been fixed by some magician of a plastic surgeon.

Dusk settled all around them. The woods that fronted Highway 20 were deepening with shadows. The sky was alive with the flitting silhouettes of small birds. They picked up the boat in Cousin Town and by the time they got to Moss Bluff they had almost no light left.

Lorene backed the trailer down the clay-banked levee with little trouble, as though she were an old hand at it. Owen waded into the cool water and cranked Crosby's boat loose. Everything felt slow and easy now; the small flat-bottomed bass boat slid with amazing lightness through the water. He dragged the bow onto the bank.

He pointed beyond the silver line of a small pumping station and dam that spanned the road to a cluster of trees. "Park the car over there. See if you can get it all the way into the trees."

To go downriver to the camp, Owen used the smaller electric trolling motor. With the stiff current, the motor moved them along at a good clip, and it was best anyway, he thought, to make as little noise as possible. He used Crosby's frog-gigging lights to navigate.

When they got hung up in hyacinths, he cut the lights and engine and leaned over the stern to free the prop. Lorene lay back along the seat with her arms folded under her head.

"Look at all the stars," she said reverently. "It's like when I was a kid." They stayed tied up there for a few minutes and listened to all the night sounds chirping and screeching around them.

He missed the point where the trail met the river the first time, but found it easily on the way back. He dropped Lorene on the bank and told her to wait and for God's sake not to get spooked and wander off.

"I'll be a few minutes," he said.

"Where are you going?"

"To stash the boat."

She watched the two elevated balls of light in the bow of the boat hum into the darkness, then break away into a ramble of bushes. The sound of the motor stopped and an alarming silence chilled her. What have I gotten my sorry ass into, she thought. She looked up at the magnificent speckle of stars above the tree line. She could hear Owen tramping through the woods toward her, and though she knew it was him, she thought bear too. A big lumbering hunk of black fur, frothing white at the mouth, with razor claws. She repeated Owen's words: Don't get spooked. She wanted to call to him to make sure that it was indeed him.

"Lorene." She heard her name as a concentrated whisper.

"Here," she shouted back.

He had something white in his hand.

"What's that?"

"A T-shirt," he said. "I'll tie it up in the morning."

He took her hand as she climbed the mud-slick rise and followed him down the trail. "Besides," he said, "I don't want him showing up with any surprises before I'm ready."

"Won't he see the boat when he comes?"

"I gave him instructions to come from the other direction."

The mud was thick on their shoes and she fell behind. He missed the insecure grip of her hand in his. She was cursing and had bent down to remove her clogs. He said, "You know, they say snakes always get the last person."

She picked up her clogs and ran to him. He laughed, then turned around, offering her his back. "Hop on."

"Gladly," she said, wrapping her arms around his neck and her heels into his groin.

"You're choking me."

"Sorry." She clasped his shoulders tightly instead.

He wanted to tell her to let up on his left one but he was

198

afraid she'd get down altogether. It felt good to have this woman's body pressed on him, even if this was the only way to get it. The pain of the talons was a small price now.

As soon as they got to the camp, he built a raging fire in the stone-rimmed pit he had dug on Monday. Brilliant amber flames lit the tent—squat and orange and surrounded by the rain ditch. His pack, draped with the rain poncho, still hung from the limb of the live oak. At first glance, it could have been a lynched man and Lorene gasped when she saw it.

One end of the tent had fallen in and Owen fixed it by replacing the stake in the ground and cinching the rope tightly.

"What's in that?" Lorene asked. She pointed to the pack but would not look at it.

"Food mostly. You hungry?"

"Scared," she said. She dug a smooth rock out of the dirt, dusted it and set it close to the fire. She folded her legs under her and sat watching the flames.

"I'll fix us something to eat as soon as I get everything straight around here." He could feel the Seconal slipping away from him now. The pleasant fog he had been in for so much of the afternoon was beginning to fade, as though the sun were finally burning through. He was tempted to ask her for another. They made things so much easier.

He tested each of the four ropes that secured the tent to the ground, then ducked inside.

"You can use this," he said, dragging the sleeping bag out of the tent. He removed the clothes he had rolled in it at Crosby's, grabbed the bag from the bottom and shook it. When he looked at her, she had her knees drawn up to her chin and her arms wrapped around her shins.

"If you're cold," he said, throwing her the flannel shirt from the bag, "put this on."

"Thanks."

He spread the bag out neatly inside the tent and turned back the top so she would only have to slide in and zip it up.

"This is all my fault," she said. "In a way."

She had slumped forward till her chest rested on her folded knees and her hands supported her shoulders from the dirt. She looked like she was ready to spring into the fire. "You're coming down from the pills now," he said. "So don't get depressed on me."

"Me and Donny and Paul," she said. Shadows of orange flame rippled her face.

All he could say was, "Don't think about it that way." But it had been precisely the way he had thought about it. They had all contributed in some preternatural way to create from nothing an avalanche of personal catastrophe. No, Paul, he thought quite rationally now, out of chaos comes greater chaos, not order. Order is a trick we play on ourselves, like donning 3-D glasses. Eventually, the glasses have to come off and what we've separated into layers so successfully, so mechanically, rushes in on itself like a breaking wave. That should have been the lesson imparted to the class that day, Paul. It was the truer lesson to be learned.

"Are you sure he won't come in the night?" she asked again.

"Not Donny."

Owen opened his buck-knife and cut down the pack. He spread the rain poncho on the ground for her to sit on and pulled out his grill and mess kit.

"I've got rice and fresh-canned string beans and tuna. Not a class menu, but it'll do."

"I need to do something," she said. "Let me help."

He handed her the can of tuna and the opener, then set to leveling the wood in the fire to accommodate the grill.

The nervous activity in the woods, caused by the bright territorial glow of their fire, died around them, leaving only the sound of popping cinders. A line of light smoke curled into a patch of open sky above them.

"Jesus, that's strong."

"The fire?" she said.

"The tuna."

"Smells all right to me." She pried the thick meat out of the can. For the first time in days, she was hungry. In the house, she could not bring herself to go into the kitchen and cook. But the fresh air and the smell of pine sap burning were beginning to take hold of her and she felt suddenly unburdened.

Owen filled a small pot with water from a plastic canteen and dumped in a bag of rice. He poked the fire with a stick to bring up the flames. A single vein raised on his forehead and his eyes bulged with each breath.

"I wanted to get out of stripping so badly," she said.

Her eyes, with the lids half closed, stared into the fire hypnotically. Come on, he thought, looking up to her, don't get sentimental. But the timbre of her voice had not wavered, and he found himself asking, "Why Donny?"

"The question's really, 'Why Paul?'" she said. She moved close to him by the fire while he squatted and stirred the boiling rice. "And I just jumped at the chance 'cause I couldn't take it anymore. Though it's not that simple."

He covered the pot and moved it to a cooler part of the fire, then lay back beside her on his elbow.

"Paul was my way out, but I found out soon that he wasn't what I wanted. Then Donny came along and he let me have part of my old life back without giving up the new one. You see, for once," she said, sliding around to face him, "for once I had the whole ball of wax, right in my hands. Both men. I loved and hated them for different reasons and it gave me immense satisfaction to be on top of the thing that had driven me for as long as I can remember."

"I knew that feeling," Owen said. "Only in a different

way. And I got off a little cheaper." A meanness urged him to draw down the bandage from his eye, to show her how well he knew, but he restrained himself. He slid the pack to him and pulled out a small baggie of pot, then crumbled a bud into his mess pan and began rolling a joint.

Lorene mixed the tuna with the rice and poured the green beans out without heating them. They shared a bottle of warm club soda. While they ate, he told her how he tried to free the eagle, how he too rode the crest of that driving energy. It had been like pulling a runaway team of horses to a halt. "But for that privileged glimpse of your predicament," he said, "you always have to pay."

In the fire she could see the faces of her audience. They glowed and faded along a single piece of burning wood, all neat in a row. Then all the faces became one face—the coal-blackened eyes of her father, the heavy slack jaw of Sara's half-brother, and the curved beak-like nose of Donny. She did not know why, but she reached out to touch it.

Owen slapped her hand from the flames. "Hey, what are you doing?"

She looked at him, startled.

He lit the joint from a piece of kindling. "Relax if you can. It's going to be a long night." He inhaled deeply and handed her the joint. She needed to back off from whatever was inside her more than he did and he would rather have her smoking than popping more pills.

He had enough fishing line to string several times across the opening of the trail and along the most likely perimeter from which Donny would come. He would leave the back side of the camp, which faced the densest part of the forest, open.

While Lorene smoked, he climbed the oak behind them. In the thick web of branches above her, he found his rifle. He uncovered it, and when he cocked it, she winced.

"Lorene," he said in a low voice. "Are you wearing perfume?"

She rolled onto her stomach and looked up at him in the tree. "Yes."

He wedged the rifle back into the crook between two branches and draped a vine over it, then swung down.

"You'll have to wash it off. I could smell it up there thick as a cloud. It's like a goddamned signal beacon."

"What do you suggest?"

"At the river."

"I'm not walking through there." She pointed into the ring of darkness that rimmed the camp. "Alone."

"I'll take you."

On the trail to the river, she stuck close to his back. His shoulders were slightly rounded and he held his arms close to his side. She noticed he made hardly a sound as he walked.

Before they got to the river, she said, "Owen, who are you?"

He stopped abruptly and she almost ran up his back. Then he started again, just as quickly, and she had to run to catch up.

"I don't exactly know," he whispered.

He tried not to look like he was watching while she peeled first the flannel shirt, then her own, over her head. From the water's edge, she threw each piece of clothing up to him and he folded it. He felt himself getting hard as she waded knee deep and splashed the water up to her belly.

He suddenly imagined he was a soldier going to the front in the morning and there was nothing so important as joining her naked in that water, palming her cool heavy breasts in the pale starlight. At one point, when he was setting up the camp on Monday, he realized his connection to Paul and Crosby. Now her question, "Who are you?" pricked at him; he desperately wanted to give her answers. He had

203

no past, no significant past, and he clung to Crosby and Paul because they held out some sort of hope for a future. They had offered him a piece of their lives and he had accepted without reservation. And now he was paying for that emotional investment.

Lorene squatted so the water came above her shoulders and washed herself. When she stood, beads of water glistened like so many small diamonds in the crescents of light above her breasts and the flat line of her stomach. He found himself asking, "Can I come in?"

At first he swam in large circles around her. She walked out deeper, careful not to wet the long strands of hair she had rolled and folded on top of her head. Her breasts bobbed like buoys above the water line. She realized she had said yes to his question without thinking. Then she told herself: What the hell, I've made worse mistakes.

Owen wanted to swim up close, to fit himself along the strong curve of her back, to kiss the shadowed hollows of her shoulders. The memory of the morning's fight with her, when he had her spread and submissive on the bed, made him sick with himself. He could not allow himself the same mistake again. The weak got dumped on but he would not be the one to do the dumping. If he could have found Mrs. Mac's boy, he would have apologized for throwing the snake at him. He would have apologized to everyone he ever knew if he could take the bad things back.

The steady current of the river kept moving him away from Lorene, who now swirled in the waist-deep water in pirouettes like a child trying to make herself dizzy. Her outstretched arms cut slashes in the night around her. Finally, he became tired from swimming and he sat naked on the mud bank.

"There's something about water," she said. She stopped with her back to him. "It makes me feel so free, so light."

She reeled around. "Do you think I'm hearkening back to some embryonic state?"

Her question took him by surprise. It sounded like something from Paul's mouth. He sat in a half-lotus with his knees pressed into the mud. He had been wondering at his own hard-on. In the cold of the river, it had been stiff as a branch, but sitting on the bank, it had shriveled so miserably that he was afraid she'd laugh.

"It would be a glorious state to be in right now." His words were empty, unconvincing.

"You want to hear something bizarre?" She walked slowly out of the water, raising her knees unnaturally high. Except where the meager light moved along her shoulders and up into her thick hair, the front of her body was clothed in deep shadows. "Something bizarre," she said again.

"Bizarre would be fine right now."

"I was going to be a social worker one time. I was going to work on the reservations back home in Oklahoma."

"I think you're a masochist."

"No really, I was."

"But what about what happened to you?"

"That was the only catch." They laughed. "For a while, though, I thought I had it licked and I thought I might find my own little understanding for what happened."

"Why didn't you see it through?"

"Because it was all a bunch of garbage. There was no understanding for what happened. Just like there's no understanding now."

She lay back in the mud. A small puddle of water accumulated around her navel. It was an open invitation to roll right over on top of her, but he wanted to read her right. He was tired of making mistakes and he never wanted to feel as base and self-destructive as he had that morning.

"Your turn," she said.

205

All manner of meanings ran through his mind. "For what?" he said.

"For something bizarre. And make it a good one, I'm still depressed."

"Give me a minute to think. No, I don't need a minute. This is about as bizarre as anything that could happen to a person. I met these two witches out in San Francisco once. One of them was a porno star, although I didn't know it until she invited me to the Fulton Street Theatre to see one of her movies."

"Witches qualify as bizarre," Lorene said. "Were they real?"

"I believed them and that made them real." He knew if he turned to tell her the story, he would end up staring at her tits or the fine curve of thighs. He did not know whether she meant anything by lying there. He had come to know she was different in that way.

"So what happened?"

"I had the hots for this porno queen. I mean she did things on the screen I'd never even thought before. I think now that I wanted her because she was someone I never really thought I could have."

"Enough with your fantasies," she said, sitting up. "Tell me about the witches."

He was glad he had not tried anything and he watched the slow movement of an island of displaced hyacinths in the shadows of the river. "Well, I wanted to screw this girl so bad I could taste it. I knew all I had to do was ask, but I couldn't bring myself to say the words. I even tried bumping into her in this coffee house in North Beach that I knew she hung out in. Finally, she just invited me down."

"Where she worked her strange and wild craft on you?" Lorene's voice deepened in mock seriousness.

"There was another girl there. The other witch," he said.

206

"She had a marvelous Roman face. Olive skin, long straight nose. The whole nine yards, but she was fat as hell and it turned me off. We drank some tea, and before long, the whole room was spinning about. Ashtrays flew at their command; lights flickered."

"They put something in the tea," Lorene said, confident that she had solved the whole mystery.

"At the time, it didn't matter. Then they tried to seduce me. The fat one left the room and the porno queen, who was sitting next to me on the couch, started rubbing her stockinged foot in my crotch. Her feet really smelled. Before I knew it, I didn't have any clothes on. You know what the kicker was?"

"What?"

"It didn't feel any different or any more special than anyone else."

"This isn't bizarre; it's your average run-of-the-mill dirty laundry."

"Keep your shirt on," he said. He stole a glance at her breasts. "So, anyway, I closed my eyes and pretended I was watching myself in a movie with her. She was going down on me, and at the same time, using a vibrator on herself. I opened my eyes right before I was going to come—I wanted to tell her so it wouldn't be a big surprise—and it was the fat one working away on me. I screamed."

Lorene tilted her head back and let loose a shrill cackle. "How did they do it?" she asked.

"To this day I don't know. But I swear they put a curse on me. What I didn't tell you was that I hit her. The fat one. I didn't mean to, but it happened before I could stop it. Right across the face. Anyway, I had the worst string of bad luck for the longest time after that. Until now."

He felt her hand in his crotch, felt himself hard, though he had not realized it when he was telling her the story, and he turned to kiss her.

They lay back together and he said, "But this is even more bizarre."

"Even more," she said.

For some reason unknown to him, Owen peeled the bandage from his eye and tossed it behind him into the river.

At first, they made love slowly on the bank. He touched her carefully, timidly, as if it were his first time. Toward the end, they both became frantic. She straddled him, clamping his head between her hands and arching up so that her breasts lightly brushed his chest. She saw his half-closed, scarred eye in the dim light and began violently shaking her head back and forth as she pumped up and down. A faint moan issued from her lips that sounded like crying. He rolled on top of her and she clawed his back through a layer of mud. Their feet thrashed in the water. He too arched up with each thrust, and he soaped her chest with handfuls of slick mud. Afterwards, holding each other tightly, they rolled into the river.

□   □

They dried themselves by the brilliant crackling fire, then lay out on the tarp. The heat stretched her skin tight and she noticed Owen was hard. Lovemaking had not been great, but it was good enough to make her fresh again. It had done what the pills had not been able to: for those moments, it made her feel nothing, think nothing, smell nothing but heavy mud on her chest and back and the excitement at her center. And rolling into the water, she thought, was a nice touch.

"You sleep in the tent," Owen said.

"And you? Aren't you going to sleep?" A terrible fear washed over her, raising gooseflesh on her belly. She imagined him trooping off in the darkness, like he had when he stashed the boat, only this time leaving her to face Donny all alone.

"I have to make things ready. I don't think I'll sleep."

She got up and started walking toward the tent.

"It'll be best if you sleep with your clothes on," he said.

Lorene gathered her jeans and shirt and crawled inside the tent. He watched the moons of her full ass disappear behind the flaps.

She worked her legs into the jeans and buttoned both shirts around her, then slipped into the sleeping bag and zipped it. She lay still, listening. She smelled sap burning in the fire and saw, through the distorted blur of the nylon tent walls, small flames leaping desperately skyward. A thought occurred to her with frightening clarity. She wanted to see Donny dead. It surfaced with precise slowness through layers of sadness and hatred and when the tip finally broke, when she saw that she could pin a name on Sara and her half-brother, on years of dancing in front of rooms full of bastards, on Paul's death and now Crosby's too, she let out a sigh that sounded like a moan.

"Are you all right in there?" Owen's voice trailed from a great distance and she wondered where the hell he was. He could not be near the fire.

"Yeah," she said. "But you set this tent up on a thick root."

"That's the breaks."

"I feel like bait in a trap in here, Owen. What are you doing?"

"Go to sleep."

Instead of counting sheep, Lorene ran through the faces that peopled her life. Behind her fluttering lids, it was like going through a complex indexing system. She had searched the faces so many times, trying to make desperate sense out of her life, but now she looked for that one face. Donny's. He came to her finally in the fading red lights of the Cameo.

After the second show, she had responded to a note Donny sent her. She gave the signal to the barmaid to bring him doubles and to water hers. She had danced well that night and she decided that it would be Donny who would pay her with his affections.

He began feeling her legs under the table. She told him to cut it—house rules and all. He kept offering her money and when he had gotten up to two hundred dollars, she thought: Oh hell, this might be fun. When they got to his hotel room, though, he had been too drunk to get it up. She remembered how seductively she had moved through her routine, and this joker was limp. She fondled him mechanically, but her heart wasn't in it anymore. He tried getting the money back and she told him to screw. He stumbled trying to grab her, and from the floor, threatened to get tough with her. Just another pig, she thought to herself as she left him.

And now, lying in the tent and listening to a scraping sound in the dirt, first near the tent, then on the other side of the fire, then back at the base of the oak, she was aggravated with herself for having so completely erased that asshole from her mind. This whole mess was her fault, in that way. If she could have found that piece of the puzzle the night Paul first brought him over, or on any of those occasions afterward, her life would still be whole.

And when she slept, she dreamed she had entered college. She was sitting in a classroom in the damp basement of Peabody Hall. The light green walls were stained with great arcs of yellow piss; the ceiling was low and sagged under a forest of emergency supports. Paul stood at the head of the class with glassless glasses plastered to his high forehead. His complexion was chalk-white and though his mouth was moving furiously, there was no sound. She sat in the front of the room wearing only her sequined G-string and pasties, diligently filling her pad with the nothing Paul was saying. The rest of the class was making catcalls and throwing wads of paper at her. She was continuously on the verge of crying.

Owen let the fire die while he set about readying the camp for Donny. With the shovel he had fashioned out of a branch from a cabbage palm, he dug a large hole where the trail opened up on the camp and covered it with a mat of pine straw. Then, with the fishing line he had bought from the cretin on the river, he tied off the trail at knee level. He strung the rest of the line inside the perimeter of the camp in the only directions that Donny could come from. At each opening, he dug several holes of varying deepness and covered them. When he finished, he surveyed his work. He had now a proper territory to defend, with a line of trees at his back and the ground in front of him wired and rigged with holes. The last thing he did was tie the white T-shirt to a branch on the bank where he and Lorene had made love.

As he climbed the oak and settled into the web of thick branches that hung out almost to the center of the camp, he thought of the eagle at the zoo. She too had carefully worked out the radius of her range, then sat at her perch oblivious to the tether as though she were truly magnificent and able to hunt from her eyrie.

The pack lay covered with his tarp and looked like the form of a man sleeping by the dying embers; the tent was quiet now. He wondered if Lorene was asleep. He thought of calling to her but changed his mind. The sound of her words came back to him from the trail where she asked them: Owen, who are you? He cradled his rifle and settled into the palm of thick branches.

There were answers he could have given her. Things he had done that she would have taken for who he was. He was a college student once, an activist, a construction worker, a hopeless marijuana addict, and on and on. And oh yes, he thought, throughout all this he had been an absolute coward. A man on the run. But right now, and he knew he could not explain this to her on the trail or at any other time, nor could he explain it to anyone else, right now he was some cosmic incarnation of intention. It had all come to this. As though his life had been heading for some unknown confrontation with the dark side of itself. He could not go forward and pull himself off the line, nor was there any hope in the past for salvation. He was an act, consummated in the beginning and end from the first instant, yet held in some hellish limbo—waiting for the precise moment to explode, to complete. It was a feeling so complete in itself that it strained every muscle, every nerve fiber implanted in his muscles, so that inside his body he felt like the shrill whine of a siren.

He listened intently to each sound in the woods. Twigs cracked under the light pressure of some night-stalking creature. An owl screeched hollow in the distance. He placed his hand over his right eye to check the vision of his left. He could feel the muscles strain to focus. His trap for Donny, he thought, was an order of magnitude greater than his attempt to set the eagle free. He learned something from that: There was no answer to who you were. Weighed against death, "who" was just another insignificance that led you into a mire of shit.

□   □

When Donny shut down the engine, there was an arresting stillness that settled on the river. A yellow ball of sun burned through a shroud of heavy fog. He pointed the bow of Owen's boat toward the bank and let it dig into the sand. It sent him lurching unexpectedly forward.

A crane, crouched knee deep in the water, flashed white and away. Donny took his shoes off and left them in the

212

boat. He rolled up his baggy jeans and jumped over the side. After he dragged the bow up onto the bank and tied it up, he took Owen's marker from the branch and balled it under the seat.

He had realized last night, while sitting in his dark office sipping Scotch after Scotch, that sending Georgia for the money was idiotic. But he packed it, along with Crosby's gun, in his briefcase anyway.

As he followed the path, he noted broken branches. He stepped as lightly as he could, carefully placing his foot along the outside tip and letting his weight settle to the heel. He avoided the brittle crunch of leaves by stepping on roots and cypress knees that stuck out of the ground. When he got close enough to smell the smoldering wood, he removed the revolver from the briefcase, tucked it into the back waistband of his pants, and silently left the trail.

Owen climbed down from the tree once during the night to put another log on the fire. He wanted to draw Donny in. He wanted him careless, arrogant, just as *he* had been with the eagle at the zoo. The waiting had been maddening. Each moment turned in on itself, expanding in the darkness, and each sound amplified with frightening intensity. He had tried slowing his breathing, counting, and slowing his heart too. He had held his eyes without blinking for small eternities. The dense webwork of the dark leaves above him blocked out all vision of the sky and each glowing ember became a star in his imagination.

When he heard the noise come steadily through the rising mist along the trail, then stop, his throat dried and tightened as though a pair of rough hands gripped him. The pressure rose behind his eyes and he picked up Donny's movement—dark blue and slow—through a lattice of pine trunks and high elder.

He rolled onto his belly and slid the rifle up into his shoulder. The tent was still quiet and he could see Donny making a wide crescent to come up behind it. He wondered if the eagle had heard him coming through the zoo as clearly as he now heard Donny. He was taken with a sense of his own controlled fear, pulsing hard at his temples and pounding behind his sternum, as this undefined danger—darting from tree to tree—materialized at the perimeter of his territory. He found himself reflexively squeezing and releasing the rifle's stock.

Donny moved cautiously up to the fishing line behind the tent. Instantly, he crouched and scanned the camp. He set the briefcase at his feet, then stepped over the line and looked around again, this time high into the trees, and Owen thought he had been seen.

"Owen?" Lorene said. He heard the muted sound of her crawling out of the sleeping bag. "Is that you?"

When he didn't answer, her voice choked. "Oh God, please, Owen, is that you?"

Donny's hand came around his back in one quick motion and reappeared with a gun. He crawled low along the ground to the side of the tent.

Move, goddamnit, Owen said to himself. Give me an inch. He flashed on the eagle, tawny and proud and patiently waiting for the perfect instant—that one point in time where there is no time—to descend in a thundering flurry of wings. All shadow and light and speed. He wanted to spear Donny then, make him feel the quick hot puncture as the talons sliced and curled into the muscle.

Lorene burst through the flaps of the tent at a dead run, trailed only by her own incongruous soft whimper. She had jumped the pit before the whimper erupted into a high scream and she was almost to the trail when the fishing line cut into her shins, sending her somersaulting into the dirt.

Donny rose above the sloping orange line of the tent. He squeezed off two shots at the tarp-covered pack that looked like a man. As he ran for Lorene, his ankle sank in one of

Owen's holes and sent him spinning into the stone-rimmed pit. Hot ashes exploded upward.

Owen had a shot then, but he waited, watching Donny absorbed in his own self-preserving contortions. He beat at his smoldering shirt feverishly. Owen felt an immense power in this ability to pick the time—the right time. He understood now the calculations of the eagle as it had watched him foolishly folding the tether, then slipping the blade of the knife inside the loop. He filled his chest with air and slowly exhaled. It was sweet, sweet as the smell of the pine sap and smoke that Donny had so completely disturbed.

Lorene scrambled to her feet, never taking her eyes from Donny. "Owen? God, Owen, where are you?" She backed into a pine tree that fronted the trail. "Run," he wanted to yell to her, but she seemed plastered there to that tree. Her face had gone pale with panic.

Owen squinted his left eye and drew a bead down the barrel to the side of Donny's head. His eye didn't hurt now. Nothing hurt. Not Paul, nor Crosby, nor even his own madness. When he cocked the hammer, Donny riveted. A look of utter consternation shadowed his face. He could not place the sound. He looked to the pack, then up to the tree where Owen lay. Their eyes locked immediately, and they were inextricably connected as surely as if they had breathed the same breath. Donny swung the pistol up quickly and Owen squeezed the rifle's trigger.

There was a deafening crack, as though a bolt of lightning had exploded from his shoulder and traveled out the barrel. Something inside him separated from his very center. It carried along the bullet's trajectory away from the tree in the swift dark movement of flight and descended, flashing knife-sharp talons, on Donny's recoiling figure as it settled to a lifeless heap at Lorene's feet.